CROSS COUNTRY
MURDER SONG

Philip Wilding is a journalist, writer and producer
for both radio and television. He currently lives
in London. *Cross Country Murder Song* is his
first novel.

PHILIP WILDING

Cross Country Murder Song

VINTAGE BOOKS
London

Published by Vintage 2011

2 4 6 8 10 9 7 5 3 1

First published in Great Britain by Jonathan Cape in 2010

Vintage
Random House, 20 Vauxhall Bridge Road,
London SW1V 2SA

www.vintage-books.co.uk

Addresses for companies within The Random House Group Limited can be
found at: www.randomhouse.co.uk/offices.htm

The Random House Group Limited Reg. No. 954009

A CIP catalogue record for this book
is available from the British Library

ISBN 9780099539933

The Random House Group Limited supports The Forest Stewardship
Council (FSC), the leading international forest certification organisation. All
our titles that are printed on Greenpeace approved FSC certified paper carry
the FSC logo. Our paper procurement policy can be found at
www.rbooks.co.uk/environment

Mixed Sources
Product group from well-managed
forests and other controlled sources
www.fsc.org Cert no. TT-COC-2139
© 1996 Forest Stewardship Council
FSC

Printed and bound in Great Britain by
CPI Bookmarque, Croydon CR0 4TD

*This book is dedicated with
much love to Ted Millington and The Boy*

Box

Tell me about the box they kept you in, he said.

I remember the darkness, he replied, and the smell of the wood and the dust. When they first put me in there I sneezed and my sneezing made a dog bark and then someone shouted shut up, but I didn't know if they were shouting at me or at the dog.

He glanced up at the therapist seated just behind him then wriggled so that he was sitting up. He still felt uncomfortable lying on his back for too long. He understood that it was meant to relax him, but it put him on edge. He looked at the blue expanse of sky through the large window at the end of the office, imagined being in an airy square somewhere with the breeze prickling his skin and exhaled deeply and slowly to stave off the panic as he'd been shown.

The therapist was looking out the same window, his pencil flat on his notepad. Are you okay? he asked. We don't have to talk about the box if you don't want to.

It's okay, he said.

They'd kept him in the box for three days. It was oily; sludge filled one of its corners and the wood splintered easily. It had a hinged door and light came in as a thin slice of gold. It smelt musty, as if it had lain empty and unused for months before it became his.

He followed the day as it progressed slowly across his chest, traversing his body and then drifting into darkness, snuffed out as the earth spun and moved him away from the sun.

When they'd first placed him in there he'd had a blue canvas bag over his head. He'd heard the lid slam shut behind him and the rattle of a chain being drawn around the box and then a lock clicked into place. He was face down, his arms tied behind his back, he couldn't control the breaths that were coming from him in bursts; he gulped and gulped as if his face were being pushed down into a shallow pool. The chain rattled into life again, the lid flying open, someone freed his hands and flipped him onto his back. There was silence, he coughed abruptly, violently, and then a hand reached into the box and quickly pulled the hood from his head; the light stung his eyes and the lid clattered shut again. Life streamed out of him in snot, tears and wheezing air.

The therapist was writing something down in his notebook, he could see it in his peripheral vision. Sometimes the therapist leant forward attentively (to an onlooker it might have seemed like he was about to touch the head of his patient, perhaps to comfort him or ruffle his hair), other times he sat back deeply in his chair, his legs crossed, tapping his pencil distractedly against his bottom lip.

You were ten, said the therapist.

Just, he replied, my birthday was a couple of days before.

He was tall for his age, taller than his friends. Taller than the kidnappers might have gauged judging by the length of the box. He could never quite stretch his legs. It was narrow too. Years later he surmised, given the oil on his clothes and the cheapness of the wood, that the box must have housed car and truck parts before it held him.

I was more worried about the chains, he said.

The chains? said the therapist.

The ones wrapped around the box, he replied. I thought they were going to throw me into a lake and the chains were to stop the box floating away, to make sure it sank. I was a poor swimmer anyway.

When did you stop worrying that they were going to drown you? said the therapist.

I didn't, he replied, not until my father came to get me.

And water now? said the therapist.

Water's okay, he said. I like swimming now.

The air conditioning hummed. Outside a car caught its gears on the hill, the engine straining against the incline.

Do you remember it happening? said the therapist.

Happening? he asked.

When they kidnapped you, said the therapist.

I remember the car coming up behind me; I remember thinking that it was going way too fast, he said. I always imagine fast cars are going to lose control, the idea scares me. I remember

3

thinking that when I heard the kidnappers' car. I didn't know they were kidnappers then, though.

Why do you think fast cars are automatically going to lose control? asked the therapist. For once his question didn't seem perfunctory. It sounded like he really wanted to hear the answer.

When I was young, he replied, six or seven maybe, I'd been out walking with my mother in town. She'd gone shopping and taken me with her, I don't know where my nanny was. She'd parked and we were waiting to cross the street.

Where was this? said the therapist.

Here, he said, in New York, we were on East Houston Street, heading for the shops in SoHo. My mother liked it down there, I did too.

And what happened? asked the therapist.

We were about to cross the road when a car came racing around the corner. I remember the noise more than anything else: the way the brakes were screeching, the tightening at the heart of the engine, the hopelessness of it all, the way the back end of the car tilted, drifted away and then came back into line. It looked like the paintwork was wet, like the car was being stretched. Like when you see those photos of pool balls on impact, and they're elongated for the briefest of moments before gravity or whatever it is snaps them back into shape, makes them spherical again. Do you know the pictures I mean?

The therapist nodded, he did.

That was how it looked, the car looked longer, like it was alive. Then it was gone and I heard the police sirens coming along after it. I remember the lights and the wailing getting louder and louder and my mother's hand tightening around mine. I tried to pull away, but she just dragged me closer and then the police car veered and dipped and never straightened again. It shunted a car on the corner, crumpling the wing. I remember the wing mirror twisting off and popping into the air and then the sound of glass breaking and a cloud of silver dust. The car they'd struck jumped back as if trying to get out of the way and then the police car bounced up off the kerb and hit the corner of a restaurant. The driver wasn't wearing a seat belt, who did then? Though I thought a cop might . . . he was on our side as they hit. I remember the jolt as he sprung upwards in his seat and his face collided with the windscreen; he looked really surprised as if he'd just come to, sitting there. His nose was bleeding and he was holding his head in his hand, tentatively, like he was scared of what he'd find if he touched it too closely.

What happened? said the therapist.

I don't know. The crowd gathered around the police car and my mother led me away; I think they were okay, I don't think the car blew up or anything like that, there weren't suddenly flames everywhere if that's what you're thinking.

The therapist glanced at him. That isn't what I was thinking, he said. He wrote something else in his notebook and stole a glance at his watch as he was doing so. So when you heard the speeding car coming up behind you the day you were kidnapped, your first reaction was to run? he asked.

No, not run, he said, almost the opposite. It used to make my legs seize up, I'd feel like I was about to flinch. It was like I was expecting the impact and I didn't want to draw attention to myself in case that made me a target.

He remembered thinking that the car was driving up too quickly behind him and stealing a glance over his shoulder, his head low as if to duck an oncoming blow. He remembered the shouting, someone's hand on a car horn, another voice telling them to shut the fuck up. He saw Karl his bodyguard being hit with a wooden club, the air leaving his body as he barrelled forward, his hands scrabbling emptily as he fell. There was already a welt raised on one side of his face, the bruising mimicking the shape of the club; the two men kept hitting Karl as he went down and then kicked him as he lay there. Then someone had hit him across the back of the head, he felt sick and scared as if the police car had mounted the kerb and clipped his calves, dragging him underneath the wheels. Then he was laid out across the back seat of the car, the sky rolling above him through the oblong of the rear window. They were pulling hurriedly away and he thought about the getaway car he'd seen on that day with his mother, with the muscular bodywork flexing into life as it raced away from the crime scene, like cars he'd seen in films. He lay there while someone sat on his legs and waited for the inevitable police sirens to start up in their wake.

And did they? asked the therapist.

I don't know, he said. They covered my head with a bag and then we pulled over somewhere and they put me in the trunk.

He was standing suddenly and someone was pushing him from behind. He fell to his knees on to grass and then was pulled to his feet again. Come on, up, a voice said, and then he was hoisted over someone's shoulder and lowered gently (almost tentatively he'd think later) into the trunk of the car. He smelt the rubber of the spare tyre and the damp permeating the soiled tartan rug beneath him. Watch your legs, said the voice, and he instinctively balled himself up as the daylight shrank to leave him in isolation.

What do you remember after that? asked the therapist.

The box, he said, the disused garage and the box, more the box than anything else.

The therapist was quiet behind him.

After I got out of there I used to have this dream where I was in the kitchen in my father's house, he said. It was late and the house was quiet and I was getting milk when I heard my father coming in so I climbed into the fridge to hide.

The fridge? said the therapist.

It was a dream, he said. It was one of those old fridges, white and tall with a steel handle to lock the heavy door into place and stop the cold air from seeping out. It was the same one that we had at the house.

And you hid in it, said the therapist.

I hid in it, he replied. I had my dressing gown and pajamas on but my feet were bare and cold. I was standing on my tiptoes to alleviate the pain and I had the belt of my dressing gown in the door so it wouldn't shut. I could see my father and his friends sitting at the kitchen table, they were smoking and talking and my father got a bottle of whisky down from one of the cupboards. I remember my father asking if anyone wanted a glass of milk instead and they all laughed. They were talking about me, how they'd rescued me.

What were they saying? asked the therapist.

I don't know, he said. One of them made the shape of a gun with his hand and fired it off at something one, two, three times and they all laughed at that. Then someone mimed karate-chopping someone and that got a big laugh too.

Did you know what your dad did? asked the therapist.

Not then, he said. My mother always told me he was a businessman. That's what everyone's dad was at my school, a businessman.

What happened in the dream then? asked the therapist.

The kitchen was quiet and my dad was clearing the glasses away, he said. Turning the lights down, emptying the ashtray and then he came towards the fridge. I'd left the milk out, but I hadn't noticed until then. My dad was holding it and then he saw my belt caught in the door. He said, what's this? He pulled it loose and held it up before him and stood looking at it and then he leant forward and locked the fridge door shut and the light went out and all I could feel was the cold on the soles of my feet.

And then? asked the therapist.

Then I'd wake up, he said.

It's an understandable dream given what you went through, said the therapist.

You think? he said, his glance was suddenly venomous. Try telling that to a ten year old.

Can you remember the last time you had the dream? the therapist asked.

Two nights ago, he said.

Eventually his father came to get him. He'd developed a pattern of sleep or near sleep by then, like a long-term patient coming to terms with his hospital ward, almost oblivious to his surroundings. Even when he was awake it was in a listless, half-conscious state; as though scales were growing over his eyes. He felt the panic filling the room, jolting him to life; someone he didn't recognise pulled the lid back on the box and made to grab his arm until someone else shouted to leave him and the box was closed again. He lifted the unlocked lid slowly and peered out. The room was empty, the far door stood open and he saw someone run past. He heard a shotgun thunder into life and more shouting and then the short, furious pitch of handguns, the sound ricocheting sharply off the concrete walls. He heard his father's voice and it made his stomach tighten. Through the open door he could see his father talking to someone slumped on the floor. Then he knelt next to them, took a knife from his pocket and made a sudden, violent upward movement with his hand and the figure shook and then was still. He closed the lid and then his father was gently opening it and pulling him towards him, saying his name.

Do you remember anything about being rescued? said the therapist.

Nothing, he said. Just my father taking me from the box and then carrying me outside and taking me home to my mother.

The therapist's alarm pinged quietly and they both stood to face each other. The therapist took his hand and held it as he spoke.

I think we're making real progress, he said, I think you're really coming to terms with what happened to you. You okay? he asked. He nodded and pulled his jacket off the coat stand and made his way past the receptionist and took the elevator seven floors down to the street. His car was waiting for him; his driver held the door and they exchanged the briefest of glances as he got into the back.

Just home, he said. He felt tired and without resolution. They drove south through traffic and out to the city's borders, the cars thinning out around them with each mile.

When his mother had died from cancer he was nineteen and away at school. His father died broken-hearted just over two years later. He'd stood head bowed at the grave, his estranged sister at his side. It had taken death to bring her back into his life. She'd left home a long time before, refusing to blinker herself when it came to the machinations of his father's business. She was older and at war with the world, and at college and rattled by the guilt she felt for her privileged upbringing on the broken backs of others, she'd cut the family free. His father wouldn't have her name spoken in the house after that, he'd rage and snarl if it came up, but they all knew it was only to hide the hurt he felt.

The day of the funeral the rain beating on his umbrella had drowned out the words of the priest's eulogy. He still wondered what he'd found to say about a man who had bullied his way through the world. He travelled back to the house alone, his sister taking a car to the station; he waved at her through the window, the water smearing her features. At the wake, his father's friends gathered around him and he recognised some of them from the disused garage; he'd caught sight of them over his father's shoulder carrying the dead bodies into the back of the building, into the shadows. One hugged him especially hard and lingered there looking into his eyes as if searching out the damage caused that day.

He was a good guy, he looked out for you, was all he said before crossing the room to grasp someone else's arm.

* * *

The drive up to the house was long and cut between the extensive gardens and the lake. His mother had loved it here, this stately pile set as an absurd notion in the New Jersey countryside. We should get a butler, she'd joke, but there were always enough of his father's men around to fetch them anything they might need.

He let himself in through the kitchen at the back. He rarely used the main doors, they were too unwieldy, too imposing, he always expected someone to be standing at the foot of the stairs announcing his name whenever he came through them. He walked into the main hall, checked the post and a note from the housekeeper who travelled out from the suburbs three times a week to administer to his and the house's needs. She'd used his credit card for groceries and to pay the gardener. He looked out at the immaculate gardens reaching into the distance; worth every cent, he said to himself, folded the note and put it in his pocket.

He went into his study, reached down to the bottom drawer of his desk and unlocked it. Inside it were two handguns and a bunch of keys on a bronze ring like a school janitor might keep. He took the keys and closed the drawer. He went down the stairs and back into the hall. Beside the heavy gilt frame of an oil painting of the house was the cellar door. He selected a key and undid the padlock and then unlocked the door itself. The cellar was vast even in the gloom; he turned on the lights and the room lit up in stages, the overhead lamps buzzing into a white glare as squares of light brought every corner into stark relief. The back wall was set with tall racks of wine reaching nearly to the ceiling, a stepladder set against its corner. There was a workbench and tools and in the corner nearest to him

11

were six boxes, matching oblongs of cheap wood with hinged doors. Two were open and empty, the other four bound with heavy chains and padlocks. He walked towards them; the figures inside were asleep, one stirred as he laid a reassuring hand on the lid. Hello, said a very small voice inside, as if in a dream. He shushed gently and put himself between the overhead light and the box to shield it from the glare. He stood there for a moment enjoying the stillness, his hand resting against the rough wood. He breathed deeply, traced a finger over the heavy links of the chain; and closed his eyes.

At the top of the stairs he turned out the lights and waited for his eyes to adjust to the darkness so he might make out the boxes once more. He pulled the door to and cupped the padlock and secured it into place. He waited there a moment and listened for the police sirens to start up, but everything was still. He walked towards the study, taking the stairs two at a time. Once there, he laid the keys on his desktop, tore a sheet of paper from his notepad and wrote a note to his housekeeper in pencil. He placed it on his desk and secured it with the ring of keys, they jangled pleasingly as he set them down. He turned to go and then paused, squatted, opened the drawer, took one of the handguns and pushed it into his waistband. He stood and admired the line it made in his reflection in the picture window. He picked up his bag as he left the room, whistling absent-mindedly as he took the stairs. He swung the expansive front door wide open and stepped out into the sunshine; someone had been kind enough to bring his car around for him. He threw the bag in the back seat, put the house behind him. Pointed the car west and drove.

Song 1: Fallen

The wind came at him at an angle, almost knocking him off his feet. The upturned colander on his head let the rain through, soaking his skull and pouring into his eyes. Should have taken the saucepan, he muttered to himself, but when he'd placed it on his head in the kitchen at home he couldn't find an angle to suit him. The handle stuck out awkwardly at the front and drew his eyes to a point, made him cross-eyed, but then when he switched it back or to the side he felt like he was wearing a baseball cap propped back on his head. It didn't feel like it had the impact he needed, it didn't suit the gravity of the situation. He caught sight of his reflection in the overhead ceiling lamp, his image even more stretched and absurd. He snatched the pot from his head, reaching for the colander with his other hand.

He clanked and clanged in the wind. The sheets of tin and steel hanging off him in irregular oblongs and squares bounced and hummed against his ribs. One piece of sheeting kept catching him below the knee, causing him to wince and curse with the impact. It was dark, the winter night chasing the light blue out of the day with the promise of a night that threatened to keep falling. The field had belonged to his father; he was at its upper point, a slight rise set at one corner abutted by the right angle of a wooden fence. He held his arms out like he'd seen scarecrows do, scarecrows in this very field, but the weight of the dozens of iron rings on each arm and the working gloves, fingers riveted into place with small badges of protective steel, and the two squares of tin hanging on strong string from each arm pulled his determination down. From a distance he looked like he might be trying to fly, but in truth he could barely raise a steel-toed boot. The wind buffeted his body; the rain dashed itself against his makeshift armour. In the distance, miles away in the black sky over the nearest town, his town, somewhere over the gabled roof of his house, the clouds broke to reveal a small window of stars and then engaged again as he waited patiently for the heavens above him to splinter with white light, to judge the distance before the lightning was drawn inexorably to earth, to spear the field at his feet. A trail of knives, forks and spoons led away from him. He counted to ten before the brightness burst through the darkness, defining the edges of the sky as it flared and died. As if on cue he thrust himself forward, chin outstretched; rising up on his toes. He looked like an athlete bearing down on the finishing line, trying to win a race.

* * *

There was no such thing as the Space Race when he bobbed above the Earth in his miniature capsule that caused him to crouch as he entered its door. He could stretch out both arms and place his flat palms against each curved wall. If he unbuckled his harness he'd float little more than a foot or two upwards in the anti-gravity air before gently colliding with the control panels above him. As the 1950s faded, America was exploring the stars, firing rockets into the night sky, denying sightings and keeping a wary eye on their Russian counterparts. In 1946 America had sprung life on the Cosmos, shooting fruit flies at the night sky a full eleven years before the Soviet Union sent a dog into orbit. While he hung there in space he had often wondered if the dog had felt the loneliness he felt; strapped into her harness, electrodes attached to her chest, food and water just in reach. She'd been a stray rounded up on the streets of Moscow. They called her Laika, it translated as Barker in English. Funny, he thought, the things you remember. She was three when they gave her up to the sky. A cross-breed, a mongrel, mostly Siberian husky they said. The American press nick-named her Muttnik and she'd died within days, two thousand miles away. He thought about her tracing her line around the Earth as he made his own lopsided circles through space. He caught sight of himself in the blackness of the glass, his image rebounding back to him as the night became its own void, always still yet always falling away. He wondered about the scientists who had sent Laika here, if they'd embraced her, tears filling their eyes, as they loaded her into the capsule, knowing they weren't going to be bringing her back?

He'd left quietly at two in the morning, a lone silver figure on the slick tarmac under the floodlights, the gleam of his domed helmet ricocheting crosses of light. He turned to wave as he entered the tip of the rocket, but there was no one to wave to – the remote figures in the control tower were hazy and a long way off – so he made do with shaking the hands of the lieutenant and his assistant who were helping him board. There was a reassuring grip on his shoulder as he was pulled tight and then the satisfying click as he was locked into place, the door closing with a gasp, cocooning him into the vacuum. He lay there, knees raised, appraising the darkness before him. There were no stars to see, but somewhere up there was a point he and his ship were already allied to. The voices murmured in his ear, he heard someone say good luck, someone else said break a leg and there was a round of good-natured laughter. Then the world was shaking and smoke obscured his view, but his eyes were already closed as he was raised heavenward, a slight cylinder easing upwards leaving a trail of flames, like torches spiked across the night showing the way, before the rocket was gathered up, leaving only wonder for those who might have seen it pass.

He was to stay there for three days, looking out on the encroaching darkness, while they recorded his heart rate, checked his blood pressure, made calculations and wrote them down, dissected him, recorded earthly things as he paraded high above them, above the shimmering glow of the world. He'd fall into a stupor momentarily, be with his family, standing with his father looking out across his land, spot crows circling overhead, wary of the static figure in the field below. Nights they'd sit out on the step of their farm and watch storms crash into the land around them. Bolts of lightning careening into the crops, corn bending with the weight of the rain. He'd bow his head involuntarily as the sky shook, he thought he'd never get used to the sound of thunder. He'd jump and his dad would chuckle and lay his hand on his head and pull him close. The earth, he'd say, never smells as good as once a storm's passed. His father would stand there the next morning, a silhouette against the sun, head tilted back, feeling the warmth of the day on his face. He'd take a breath and hold it, letting it go with a sigh.

The Indian Ocean was below him; he recognised it from his sheaf of maps and charts, its shape at least. It glimmered invitingly and he wanted to be up to his shoulders in its warm waters, gazing up into the pale blue that folded up into the darkness that held him. When he'd first flown jets at the edge of space, at the edge of the sky, he'd seen the orange light flatten out into shades of blue, azure and purple and into black. He had forced himself to hold his line, wanting to wrest himself away from the precipice, maintaining his position between heaven and earth until the voice in his earpiece called him down, letting him drop his wings and fall back to the familiar criss-cross of runways that signalled the approach of his base. When they told him they were sending him into space, he had felt elation and fear. He'd seen the stratosphere, said the Colonel across the desk, now it was time for him to reach out and touch it. Exosphere, he'd told him, not stratosphere, he'd be touching the exosphere. The Colonel had creased his brow and pushed the envelope filled with his orders at him and he'd left the office without another word. At home he'd sat at his kitchen table, the papers fanned out before him, Confidential stamped across every page. He stroked a bottle of beer distractedly, making notes and doodles in the margins. It broke down into three simple parts; take off at night, orbit the planet for seventy-two hours – his vital signs tattooed back to earth by electrical impulse – then land in the ocean off the Florida coast just before dawn where they'd fish him out of the sea and, debrief him for days. He was promised leave afterwards, but in the confines of the camp, in case they needed to keep an eye on him. You never knew what could happen, they said, to the first American in space.

His father spoke to him first. He was upside down when the voice filled the capsule. He looked up and realised he was looking down towards the earth, inverted in his seat. It was morning and the sky outside was glowing which meant that snow had fallen overnight. His bedroom was white as if the flakes had seeped in at the ceiling's joists and settled in deep drifts. His father was outside calling his name, Joe, Joey, get out here. He looked out of the window, his father's footsteps leaving tracks that led away from the house into the cornfield to the west. The sun on the snow dazzled him; he thought he could see his father waving, his black jacket, the red hat he pulled onto his head almost every time he stepped out of the door, a gloved hand making a wide arc in the air, then the corn rustled as he disappeared among its long stems. He was outside now, each crunching step leading him to the perimeter of the field. Far above and below the African continent drifted by, the distant sun striking his capsule as its beams reached down to bake the ground. The light hurt his eyes even behind the reflective pane of glass that dominated his helmet. He stepped into the corn and was lost, each time he pulled a stalk aside snow fell into his hair, onto his hands. He'd forgotten his gloves, his hat, his bunched fingers were already pink and numb.

He pushed his way in, light breaking through momentarily as the dense swathes of the tall, pale grey crop moved aside, closing behind him with a crack, shuddering and upright, resuming their unwavering stance. What ocean was that? He was losing his bearings. His father was standing before him as his capsule turned into the brightness of the sun, the yellow light burning into white. His father was saying something to him, pulling him close, the corn behind him, he reached out to touch his father's face, a child's hand on his ruddy cheek, the wind picking up, everything drawn in detail. His father's hand covering his own, you're cold, he said, and pulled him close. The sun became engorged and huge, bearing down on both of them, everything consumed, glowing like hot coals, the quickly melting snow and then a rumble and clap and the searing flash of burning white and then they were gone leaving just the corn and the crows above picked out like small black crosses scratched on the great steel plate of the sky.

They pulled him out of the sea around four thirty in the morning, minutes behind schedule. He told them drowsily he admired their timekeeping as they carried him from his craft to theirs. He saw his capsule rising from the choppy waters; it looked minute even when wrapped in chains; they were already covering it with heavy tarpaulin, secreting it away. It would undergo as many tests as him over the next few days. He felt the sway of the boat, the low thrum of the engine making headway towards the coast. Then he was in the air, the swish of the helicopter's blades making hazy revolutions above him. How's he doing? asked the pilot, looking back at him over his shoulder, his black visor covering his eyes. He's doing great, someone said, and he wondered if it were true.

Three days later and the base psychologist was looking over his testimony, eyes momentarily distracted from the page, assessing him over the top of the file he was holding. His eyes darting across the page, then a flicker of curiosity and he'd appraise him again, as if staring across at him might suddenly reveal an insight missing from the information he had been given. Your vital signs were all good, he said, laying the file on the table, his hand tapping distractedly on its cover. The things you said you saw, no irregularities even then, nothing untoward, nothing out of the obvious. The windows were frosted, the sound of the base outside; the drone of trucks and jeeps, the call and return of conversation, someone said sir abruptly, aircraft buzzed by. The office was still, however; the psychologist wore a white coat as if they were in lab conditions.

What do you think you saw out there? he said. I don't know what I saw, he replied. It might have been a dream, I suppose. I had no concept of day or night, up or down. He didn't think it was a dream though, but now he wished he'd never mentioned his father, his figure filling with light, how the interior of the capsule became so bright that he felt the light passing through his eyelids and filling his skull. He'd filed his report, told them of the hours spinning in space, the feeling of weightlessness, the earth from above, the ache of solitude, how the heavens made him feel cold even though his body temperature remained consistent throughout. He didn't tell them that he'd been scared, terrified of the windows of his ship splintering in their frames, the pressure worrying his skeleton down to nothing, his eyes being forced deep into his head. Machismo had made him wary of telling them about that, but touching his father's face, being suspended in space, feeling elation then the terrible loss, he thought that might be important, that every journey might cost more than toil, than money, that you might have to pay with something intangible, that you might have to give of yourself.

The universe, he said to the psychologist seated opposite him, it might take as well as give. He told him about the emptiness, about the new hollow at the core of his being and the wonder he found out there among the stars. And while they talked, the doctor nodded and made agreeable noises in the back of his throat and his hand dashed across his notebook taking everything down.

He was formally discharged three months later. They draped him with honours, guaranteed him a pension for life and made him write his name on dozens and dozens of sheets of paper. His endless looping signature guaranteeing his silence and his loyalty. The colonel told him he was sorry to see him go, but he couldn't hide the surprise in his eyes when he saw how much weight he'd lost. Later, he'd ask if the pilot's shrinking frame had anything to do with the space flight and he was told that they didn't know for certain, that it would take time, that it might be the grief that was causing him to fade. Grief? said the colonel. The mission was a success, what did he have to grieve over? They didn't know, they said, they just didn't know.

At home he sat at the kitchen table, staring with new wonder at the night sky. He could still hardly believe that he'd been pinned up there among the stars, gazing down onto this planet. He wished that his father would come at night while he slept, that the blaze would reignite in his head and carry him home. The sky flickered at the corner of his eye like a light switch going on and off. The fragmented bolts of lightning coming down in shards towards the earth. He hurried outside instinctively, like a dog sensing a stranger in the yard. A heavy rain was beginning to fall; he felt it on his face, the weight of it in his hair. Another flash and the serrated edge of a distant tree-lined hill was backlit and then quickly shrouded in the darkness. The sky roiled and thundered, the rain became more insistent. He ran to his kitchen, grabbed a bucket and started emptying cutlery and pans into it. Next he went out to his work shed, grabbing sheets of tin, a ball of string. He rattled around picking up squares of sheet metal, oblongs of iron, he pulled the metal panelling off his back door, throwing it all into the back of his truck. He pulled out on to the road, each rut and bump made his pickup jangle.

He stood exposed, forcing pieces of tin into the waist of his trousers, securing it into place with his belt, tightening it around his chest. He placed the colander on his head, cast knives and forks and spoons around his feet, strapped pieces of corrugated iron to his arms. He felt tethered to the earth, moored in place. The energy came up in waves from the ground, the dense corn fanned out, almost flattened by the wind. He counted to three and the flash of light rose up before him, a giant curtain obliterating the night. He heard his father, saw him follow on in the jagged lustre. The sky reared up and the rain drove him back one faltering step, but he thrust his chin forward, an antenna tuning the universe in.

Chorus

The driver of the car was lost, his wipers leaden against the deluge he was navigating his way through. The sky crackled, his radio babbled momentarily and was suddenly mute. He slowed, though didn't quite stop, the road a morass of gravel and mud beneath his wheels. He leant forward trying to make out the way ahead when the light flooded through the car, and to his left, like a model posing, caught in the flashgun's glare, he saw the figure reach out, beseeching the sky, then the air embraced the earth, the sky held itself to the ground, he clutched the wheel as the sparks rose in plumes and something exploded. Then it was dark again. His headlights picking out the road ahead, he flicked them to full beam to stave off his creeping fear as he began to imagine figures rushing up at him from the darkness, clambering over his car, blotting out the windows with their bodies.

When he was younger his family had spent an afternoon at a safari park, driving through fenced enclosures filled with dormant tigers and supine buffalo, the animals grazed leisurely, casting an occasionally curious glance at the families ferrying past at a sedate pace. He'd enjoyed it until they'd coasted to a halt and a family of monkeys had thrown themselves at their car, clinging to the roof, springing happily up and down on the hood. They pulled at the door handles, hung cheerfully upside down from the roof and inspected the startled occupants behind the glass. His father had loved it.

Will you look at these fucking things; he beamed, until their mother had glared him into silence.

Ah, sorry kids, his father said, *forget I said that,* and he turned in his seat and gave them a wink.

He looked back to the window only to let out a startled yell as a monkey loomed in to lick the glass. He sat back sharply, accidentally jolting his sister who pushed hard back, then they were squabbling, the car pulling away filled with the sound of sibling rage and their mother demanding they calm down. The monkeys slid off the slowly moving hood and roof, leaving the windscreen wipers mangled and useless. One pair linking hands, then walking in a strangely high-stepped fashion back to their climbing frame, scratching themselves absent-mindedly as they went.

From the sky the whole country looked like a map; a clean grid of roads running east to west, north to south. Parallel lines, straight, unremitting points from A to B. That's how the driver saw it when he closed his eyes and thought about the journey stretching out before him. One unrelenting path leading from the Jersey Shore to the edge of the New World and into the Pacific Ocean. The reality though was rutted streets, one car wide, undulating, sandy-coloured stretches that followed the line of the hills he was traversing. Endless highways, dashed with dividing lines of yellow and white, their verges in constant motion, long, willowy grass nodding at the cars as they dashed by. Idiots no matter where you were, the squeal of tyres as someone jumped your lane, long, angry horns. Roads that defied belief as they held to the face of the hill, circling ever upward and then flattening out into a plateau with the world below stilled momentarily. Driving down towards a valley floor at night, pitching towards the distant lights, coming in like a small aircraft, unsure wheels feeling for the tarmac. Roadside barriers were blue in some places, red in others, green, black, orange, burnished steel, buckled and bent. Rushing into one unremitting span as he built up speed. Ominous spaces where a vehicle had crashed against the restraint; popped the metal shield off its posts and sailed into the space beyond. Falling out of sight, sunlight streaming through the front and rear windows, briefly catching the startled shapes of the passengers as shadows as they began their descent to the streets below. He saw the moon, giant and spectral in mountain passes, bleaching the night, the sun fierce and blinding as it rose up, lighting up the earth around him, making everything golden and bright.

The road hit a different pitch when he was travelling over water, everything up a notch as if he was freewheeling or had shifted a gear. He could almost feel the space beneath the car, the timber supports of the bridge, the gentle lapping of the river rolling below him. He enjoyed the dappled light through trees; the sunshine made him think of school holidays and early mornings when his dad had been around more, before he started appearing in the papers and solemn-faced men sat in cars at the end of the drive staring in at the house and the weather felt like it was always about to change. That the forecast was becoming increasingly gloomy.

When he turned fourteen his father got him a job at a high-end resort upstate, just over the Canadian border. Weekend Warriors (as he and his friends called them, barely suppressing their smiles) would *fly in to the private airstrip and work on their golf swing or swim in the lake. Some would take off into the woods with a guide to hunt deer. They'd come back at night and he'd see them at the bar as he was collecting glasses and clearing ashtrays, they'd be drunk and fiercely loud as if they'd conquered the wilderness single-handedly. They'd order drinks for everyone and recount how they'd stalked the doe into the undergrowth, while their guide sat behind them rolling his eyes theatrically; he'd seen the same scenario a dozen times.*

It's out there, the hunter would say, with a wave of his flabby arm, his garish bracelet rattling, indicating where the carcass was hanging. I felt alive, you know, he'd tell anyone who was listening. It was odd, he thought, how they always felt so alive amongst death. They'd usually talk themselves into a stupor and would have to be helped to their cabin at the end of the night. Come on, killer, he'd say to them as he pulled their arm over his shoulder and walked them out. He'd see them out on the golf course the next morning, absurdly dressed in checks like a cartoon approximation of a golfer and they'd wave to him as he brought towels and drinks to the teeing green, and mime drinking and the terrible hangover they were dealing with. They'd tell him he was a good guy, one of the best, and then they'd leave a generous tip on his tray and wave him away as they turned to size up their shot that would almost always veer off into the woods either side of the fairway. You'd sometimes see deer there, but not when any of those guys were playing. They knew to stay away then.

He spent three happy summers in this elite backwoods and whenever he returned after the break there would always be stories of late-season hunters lost out in the woods or of the police raiding the dope farmers who dotted the heavily wooded hills; everyone knew they were out there, but they were so deep in the firs that the authorities rarely bothered them. Occasionally, some inexperienced campers (the ones who thought the great outdoors was their friend) were attacked by bears, but mostly the bears wanted to be left alone unless they were hungry, though that was only in the winter and it was best to be off the mountain then anyway.

The traffic up ahead was slowing down, the third time it had bottlenecked that day. He turned his radio off with a stab of his finger and lowered his window, the traffic looked like it was backed up for miles. He slowed to a halt and put his head out, craning his neck, but all he could see was taillights and the backs of other heads, dozens of people unified in their stupidity, looking for something when there was nothing to see. He took a can of beer from under the seat next to him and drank heavily from it. His one concession was to keep the label hidden with his gloved hand. The kid in the car in front turned to look at him and he held the kid's gaze evenly until the boy pretended to notice something crawling on his forearm and quickly turned his attention there. Up ahead someone started leaning on their horn and then more and more motorists joined in until the air was a tangled, cacophonous mess.

Great, he muttered to himself, then leant heavily on his horn too, gulping at his beer as the noise built and built.

Song 2: Deer

Bears, he said, lifting the peak of his cap with his thumb and tipping it back on his head, need your respect.

This time of year, he indicated the banks of muddy snow bordering the road with a wave of the petrol pump he was holding, they're foraging for food, they get – he paused – quite restless. He placed the fuel pump back into its holster and went inside the little gas station and rang up their bill on an antique register. It pealed into life as rows of coloured tabs with dollars and cents written on them sprang into view.

He had wondered about hunting so late in the season. It was getting colder and before bears went into hibernation they scavenged and hunted for food (he'd read in a magazine) with a sometimes startling ferocity. Lot quicker than you think too, the guy at the store had said, regarding their bright, newly-bought hunting tunics coolly. They left, gunning the engine on their hire car, and headed towards the town on the lake. The endless-looking lake actually spanned a time zone so that the ferry either deposited you on one side at approximately the time you left the other or threw you a little way into the future as you landed. The hunting was across the water in the forest of pine that covered the glacier, a dense blanket of uniform trees that changed from bottle-green to dark brown as it followed the lip of the mountain.

They'd flown north to an area outside of Waterloo that was dotted with private airstrips and exclusive golf resorts and offered weekend hunting packages for customers from the southern cities who wanted a taste of the wilderness. As they came through the clouds to land the airport looked like it was waiting just for them. It was hectic all summer long, though the miniature terminal felt like a ghost town after September. Waterloo was set on the lake, a small, idyllic-looking town that had grown up on the logging industry. These days the local kids were caddies on the weekend and skiing or snowboarding when winter came in. Waterloo had been made briefly famous in Steve Martin's Roxanne, his cinematic reworking of the Cyrano De Bergerac legend. On the first night there they'd had to get used to cab drivers and locals pointing out plastic awnings dotted on bar and hotel windows and telling them how and where they'd featured in the film.

Steve Martin, what's he like? He a dick? he'd asked one cab driver.

Uh-uh, he said with a firm shake of his head. Real gent, and he didn't acknowledge the pair again even as they left his car, pressing a generous tip into his hand.

Daylight hours were short so the next morning they set out early, catching the first ferry across the lake. Cars honked and queued below them as they sat on the deck admiring the view. Ahead of them gently sloping hills rose out of the water and disappeared into the low sky.

Dope farmers all along there, said his companion, gesturing with his arm towards the horizon made jagged by tightly packed fir trees.

Dope farmers? he replied. Who told you that?

A friend of my brother's used to work for the DEA, he replied. They would take small spotter planes and fly grid lines over the mountains trying to spot crops. They've got camouflaged fields up there, huge barns filled with lights, they give off heat, helps them grow.

Nah, he said, warming his hands on the cup of coffee he was holding.

It's true, said his friend, a passenger plane crashed up there last winter and they sent a team in to search for survivors and stumbled on a farm; they were threatened with guns. This guy, my brother's friend, his team went in and closed it down. The guy got ten years for growing all that weed.

What happened to the other farmers? he asked. He couldn't help himself, his interest was piqued; he imagined leaving his job in the city, casting off the shackles of corporate life (he wouldn't have been able to identify a shackle if someone held one three inches from his face, but his fantasies weren't there to be hindered by reality) and giving himself over to toiling his illegal acres, his one man crusade against the war on drugs. He imagined the sweet smell filling the air, fresh dope every night, strong coffee every morning. He pictured himself walking the hills carrying some kind of staff, ducking between barns, tending his crops, then the helicopters fanning out overhead, figures crashing through the undergrowth, throwing him to the floor, shutting him down, his face in the papers looking stoic but restless, the DEA agents grinning behind him like anglers measuring their haul.

They're still out there, said his friend. Those woods go on forever and the forest's so dense, he nodded at the impenetrable green in the distance, that it's near impossible to see them from the sky. They pulled my brother's friend out eventually: they were working in there for weeks and they still got nothing except for that one guy and his crop.

They burn the dope, he said, chuckling. Imagine sitting around that bonfire.

They picked up their truck on the far side of the water and drove a rutted, single-track road up into the mountains.

Feeling every fucking bump, he muttered, his hand drifting towards a radio that wasn't there. They reached a plateau that afforded them a view to the west of the glimmering surface of the lake being lit up intermittently by a pallid sun. The rest of the valley fell away below them, green, brown and black; there were patches of white, but the night's snow had barely settled up here. Occasionally there were sprays of birds that broke the spikes of pine and threw the horizon into chaos. They packed their rifles up onto their shoulders and made the descent into the copse, each heavy step a struggle through the slushy earth. It was cold, even through their gloves; their noses were bright and pink in the freezing air.

Hey, Karl, he said, you look like Rudolph. The cold was making his eyes moist and he couldn't stop blinking. His friend hushed him. Christ, he whispered, don't go mistaking me for a deer. They crouched in spite of themselves and moved slowly forward, eyes darting left and right, as they imagined professional hunters might. They'd been hunting together since they were in their teens, at first with his dad and then once with Karl's older brother. His father had impressed upon them the importance of the hunting season and the equilibrium of the land, how nature had to have balance. He'd come to understand that, though he'd still cried when his father had first shot a deer. For his part, Karl's older brother packed beer as a necessity for their trip and when he finally felled a doe he let out a yowl like he'd won the lottery. Later, his father asked him how the trip had gone and when he told him, his father had become so angry that he'd had to leave the room. His mother stood next to him at the window, her arm around him, as they watched his father crush an empty cigarette packet and then toss it to the ground before stomping around in small circles; his features were dark, his fists bunched.

Karl, he said, your brother still a dick?

Karl nodded. Still owes me money that I lent him at Christmas, he said.

It's almost Christmas now, he replied.

Last Christmas, said Karl, like the song.

The light through the fir trees was patchy and the going slow. They'd only seen one doe. In his excitement to signal the creature to Karl, first by waving animatedly and then with one final, defeated, hissed Karl!, he had scared it away. The doe's head had twitched into life and she'd sprung away on her elegant haunches. Karl glared at him as if he'd just fallen and plunged a knife through his boot.

You're so stupid that you'd make a wax effigy of yourself to poke pins in, he said. Karl had said it before, but not for a long time, not really since school. Their bags and rifles were heavy so they stopped and sat on a fallen tree and drank water and ate their food quickly.

Remember what the guidebook said, said Karl. The smell of food can attract bears. He regarded his tuna and sweetcorn roll and thought to himself that even though bears hunted for salmon, would they know or recognise tuna let alone sweet-corn? They both wolfed their food down and then sat momentarily as their stomachs grumbled at their haste.

Remember when we saw that cub? he said.

He was eleven, Karl a year older; his father owned a Winnebago (he'd told Karl once after his father's death how much his dad had loved that Winnebago, how he thought he was a fron-tiersman when he got behind the wheel) and they'd travelled into the mountains for the holiday weekend. They'd parked up, his mother on a lounger applying suncream to her forearms, stretching her fingers out, making the skin taut, his father rooting through the back of the truck for his fishing rod, talking to himself distractedly, the radio playing.

Don't go too far, he said, his back still to them. They'd taken a ball and walked for a while, before they came upon a clearing that was washed nearly white with sunlight.

How long were we out there until we saw him? asked Karl.

No idea, he replied. They'd been kicking the red ball back and forth, trying to keep it in the air. As the ball went from foot to foot they counted the number of consecutive strokes they managed without letting it fall to the ground.

Twenty-two, he'd said, arms spread wide to give him balance

as he held the ball one-legged on the laces of his shoe. He was about to flick it back to Karl when he noticed the look on his friend's face. He could still see that face now, everything circular, his wide eyes, his open, cooing mouth, he couldn't remember him ever looking so young. He let the ball drop to the ground and turned to see the bear cub about twenty feet away. Swaying slightly, rocking gently from side to side, it raised itself up, one paw leaving the ground.

Oh, Karl had said, his mouth dropping open with delight.

He was a beauty, he said. Karl sat across from him, one hand on his stomach as if to quieten the rumbling.

His mother thought so, he said.

They'd both called out to the cub, made petting sounds and walked slowly towards the small, brown animal.

Remember the noise? asked Karl.

Do I, he said.

They weren't sure how long the trees had been moving, but they exchanged startled looks when the thrashing became too violent to ignore. The wall of trees exploded, leaves and branches bursting outwards as if they'd been fed into a thresher. The cub's mother stood between them and her cub: he could see the bubbling saliva on her teeth, her top lip quivering like an angry dog's. They stood very still, but he felt his breath expanding through his body; he wanted to quiet it. He thought it was loud enough to attract the bear's attention. His hands were numb, spreading from the tips of his fingers up to both elbows. If she attacks me, he thought, I won't even be able to cover my face. They'll find me without any of my features. They'll have to identify me through dental records. The only sound was of the bear sniffing the air and the cub giving a grizzled yawn. Then quickly the mother grabbed her cub by the scruff of its neck and shot them both a threatening glance. She retreated backwards with her dark eyes still set on them. The treeline swallowed her up, branches crackled underfoot and then nothing. They stood stock still in the moment immediately afterwards, both (as they admitted to each other later) too scared to move in case any noise might make the mother come racing back to knock them into the air like bowling pins. Then, when they could finally stand the calm no longer, they both turned and ran screaming his dad's name as they went crashing through the woods. The red ball lay half in the sun, half in shadow.

It was dusk when they finally saw the second doe. The forest was darker now and they'd talked about heading back, but had decided on thirty more minutes before going back down to the lake. Any later and they'd be in danger of missing the last ferry to take them across the water and home.

I don't want to spend the night in the truck, he said. We'll freeze our asses off. Karl quietened him with a wave of his hand; he followed his gaze and saw something moving just beyond the next line of trees. Instinctively, they both levelled their rifles and drew a bead on the shadow. He tried to slow his breathing down like his dad had taught him, but the excitement rushed through him and made his heart thud rapidly in his chest.

Hold on there, said a voice. A man, arms half raised, a rifle in one hand pointing in the air, came towards them. It's a little late to be out here, he said – and he wasn't sure if the man with the gun was referring to the season or the time of day. It was late either way, he thought.

We're not DEA. He said without thinking.

No one said you were, said the man with the gun. You look like hunters to me, he said, looking at them like the man in the store had. Any luck? he asked, but he could see that they weren't carrying any prey.

You live up here? asked Karl, though they both knew he did and they both knew he'd come from his barns and his crops nearby, from adjusting the lamps and measuring the yield. Their noise (neither was the stealthy hunter they'd like to imagine) had brought him out here.

Not too far, said the man, and he threw back his hand as if to reveal the gloom behind him for the first time. You be careful, he said, as he turned towards the darkness, it's getting on.

They were now turning into outlines and clouds of ghostly air and as if silently signalling to each other they turned and headed back up the hill towards the plateau and their truck. Neither spoke a word. Then, just ahead of them, the doe appeared; something had caught her attention, something on the forest floor, she was close enough that they could admire the ambivalent beauty in her sad eyes, the streaks of colour in her coat, her bobbed tail. Without thinking, he raised his gun and the shot broke along his barrel, the sound rising and evaporating as the deer fell.

Clean kill, said Karl, rushing forward. I knew we'd get one, he said, though they both knew that wasn't true. They kneeled over the body, Karl reaching for his knife to strip the carcass. He cut away at the coat, opening their bag to collect the meat. A friend of theirs served venison sausages and steak at his bar and anything they brought back guaranteed them a drinks tab running long into the winter. That wasn't why they hunted, though. More than one friend had asked them why they kept making the journey north and though they answered that it was the challenge and the adventure it was neither any more. Hunting brought them together at a time when new responsibilities were gently prising them apart. Each time they came out here it was to their own splendid isolation. The story of the bear cub was one they retold every time and never tired of (their friends had wearied of it a long time ago). Hunting brought them closer to a dead father and to a brother who, though wild, was then still untroubled by jail time or overhanging debts that weighed on them all. Their friendship had been forged in the crack and whip of a rifle's volley, in the animals stilled in their sights.

Karl was on his knees carefully wrapping the meat and placing it gently into the bag lying next to him.

Come on, he said, we'll miss the ferry. And then there was a noise coming through the forest, one they recognised. He felt the numbness in his fingers and the air ballooning through him, expanding in his lungs so he suddenly felt light-headed; his strangled gasps for air were making him mute and unable to move. He saw Karl and then he saw the bear towering above him, black, seemingly taller than the trees that surrounded it. Made of the woods and the night, it raised a giant paw that blotted out the sky and he imagined its claws covered with stars, a quarter moon held in its palm, and then when he looked again Karl was gone. The roaring filled his head, the stench of the doe's guts were in his mouth. He thought about running for the safety of his father's arms, but he knew his father was gone.

Later, when the man with the gun had found him and they'd

taken him down from the mountain and across the lake and listened to his delirium-filled dreams of bears cradling the night sky, they'd returned him home to the city. He remembered the doctor at his bed explaining that they couldn't save the rest of his arm, as there was no arm to be saved. The man with the gun had saved his life, he said, with quick thinking and a tourniquet.

He was growing dope up there, he mumbled, and the doctor had looked at him for a moment.

I'm sorry about your friend, he said. He looked down at his shoulder, now a neatly dressed stump.

We were hunting, he said, indicating with a nod where his arm had once been. They didn't find Karl, he said. You see, the bear was hunting too. The doctor said, if there's anything you need and then without looking back he left the room.

Waterloo in the summer was busy with tourists. He took a cab into town, praying that it wouldn't be the driver from their last trip. The plastic awnings were still in place though when someone brought up their history he smiled and nodded. He stayed at the same hotel and the next morning, as he sat on the deck of the ferry admiring the familiar terrace of distant pines and the sun skipping across the dark blue of the lake, the inexhaustible and familiar honking of boarding cars rose up from beneath him. He held the rail with his one arm, sitting with his face set into the breeze as the ferry pulled away across the water and into the past. A passenger caught his eye. Do you mind? she said, indicating the seat next to him. He shook his head and the woman sat down. They were halfway into their journey before she spoke again. Going hiking? the woman asked.

No, he said, patting the bag on his lap. I have a friend over there. He nodded towards the far shore. I'm going to find him.

There was a pause. A good friend? the woman asked.

The best, he said, shouldering his bag as he stood. Within moments he was lost among the passengers filling the deck.

Chorus

His journey westward had turned out to be less a land rush and more a slow sideways drift. He'd left home with a defiant slamming of car doors, the warm revving of his engine, leaving his life there unboxed, the contents strewn across the basement floor. He'd got lost quickly though, once he'd crossed the Hudson River he felt disorientated. Cars cut him up as he tried to take exit ramps that moment too late. He lost count of the faces he saw contorted with rage.

Breathe, Jesus, he sneered, as he pulled his car wildly to one side and on to a tributary road, pressing down hard on his horn. Eventually, more by luck than design, he found himself heading south towards New Jersey, the horizon dotted with smoky factories, planes circling over Newark Airport, some dipping out of sight, others ascending to take their place above him. The fields of grass abutting the highway were red and then shades of brown. He made a pact with himself that he'd turn right before he got as far south as Philadelphia. Then he smiled at his reflection; he'd be heading west, like a pioneer.

He returned the petrol pump to its holster and patted himself down for his wallet as he headed into the store to pay.

Are we near Milwaukee? he asked the girl serving behind the counter. It's not like we're too far east of it, right?

The short man standing next to him waved a packet of cigarettes around.

You've gone back on yourself, said the man. You're driving away from Milwaukee. He looked out the window at his car as if that might give him a clue why he might be heading east instead of west. Where you headed? he said, fingering the packet.

Towards Milwaukee, he replied. Going west, he said, silently wishing he'd stayed lost.

No you're not, laughed the man, not at all.

He paid for his gas while avoiding the gaze of the man with the cigarettes, who now seemed fascinated by him, staring up as if he were a work of art he couldn't quite understand.

He thanked the girl and exited the store and then pulled his car over to the washroom and walked in, standing in the half-light of the pebbled windows, retracing his steps and wondering where he'd got himself turned around.

Wasn't Happy Days set in the Milwaukee suburbs? he wondered. And if not, then Laverne and Shirley lived in the city. Didn't they work in the beer factory? He saw the opening titles, saw either Laverne or Shirley placing her glove onto a beer bottle as it rolled by on a conveyor belt; they both giggled, clutching hands as they ran for the door. He hummed the theme tune to himself as he stood facing the urinal and urged himself to piss.

He wasn't aware of the door behind him opening as he addressed his dick with what he imagined was an internal monologue but was actually becoming more audible with each utterance.

Come on, he reasoned, once you've finished then we can go. What does it take? I'm as full as a blimp.

His voice had gone up a note, his words increasingly urgent. By the time he'd finally got to the point where a thin stream was eking out of him he'd been bargaining with himself for more than a minute. The cough caught him by surprise, it was neither theatrical nor demanding, merely the cough of someone in a nearby stall who needed to clear their throat.

Hey, he said, imagining a smile in his voice like the ones on the radio that he'd been listening to for the last hundred miles. His mother would have said their disposition was sunny; their words chimed the time, the news and weather (even a severe storm warning or a three-car pile-up and jackknifed lorry spilling livestock onto the highway sounded like a reward in their chuckle-filled mouths). They gargled happiness as if it were green and came in a bottle. His hey was far too loud, he knew.

Hello, responded the wary voice from the stall. It sounded like the voice of a man trying to make himself small enough not to be noticed, small enough to disappear through a grille and escape outside.

You know what it's like when you've got to go, he chirruped, anything to help.

The stall was silent. The man in there would really like me to go he thought, as he wrangled his dick back into his trousers. Politeness, stupidity or a need for closure compelled him to stay; he stood outside the toilet door to make his pitch. The last thing he wanted was for this stranger to think he was odd. His mother's insistence on politeness had bordered on obsession, he imagined it was her own way of counteracting what she knew his father did in his daily life. His practices were anything but polite; his point was almost always rammed home.

So he started to explain about leaving the city and driving west, how he'd got lost in the rain as soon as he left New Jersey, how grass became a more vivid green when it was wet. He noticed the different panels of wood on the stall door, how the grains ran against each other, he mentioned this, his effusiveness knew no bounds. He mentioned how charmed he'd been by the undulating lie of the land so far, how music transformed the journey. He was getting to his point – the motivational speech he'd been making to his bladder – when there was the clink of a belt buckle, the sound of jeans being pulled up and then buttoned. He adjusted his posture, noticed the blinding light piercing the mottled glass of the half-opened window; there had been flies buzzing on the ledge, but now they were gone. It was still and silent in there, almost peaceful.

The gun was very close to his eye, a short barrel on a small gun. The hand clutching it came over the top of the stall's shortened door like a homicidal Punch doll with murder in mind. He instinctively reached around to the small of his back to retrieve his and found himself feeling blindly around like someone reaching for change that had rolled away under a chair.

Where the fuck? he whispered, eyes wide. His way wasn't the only thing he'd lost. He could make out the forehead and eyes of the man in the stall but the rest of his features were hidden behind the snub-nosed barrel of the gun. The hand holding it was shaking slightly.

Leave me alone, said the man; his voice was trembling much like the gun was trembling. He was short, his hair was thinning at the front and he had it brushed back into a fragile pompadour. He noticed the grey and blond hairs on the back of the man's hand, the opaque blue of his irises. He was blinking as if he had something in his eye.

Get out, he stammered, running the barrel of the gun swiftly across the top of the door, the rasping, scraping sound it made making them both jump a little. He felt the transference of fear crackling in the air between them, like electricity jumping in a wavering blue arc between two brass balls just like they'd shown him in school. He was suddenly filled with the bewilderment and panic he'd uncomprehendingly instilled in the man in the stall. The door opened and a gun was being waved at him, someone was shouting and he felt his thighs weaken. The air changed around him; suddenly he was bathed in light then blinded, then feeling cool air on his face.

Light, he thought, I'm dead. He imagined that in a moment he'd be able to see his bloody corpse below him as he floated away down a tunnel and into eternity. He adjusted his eyes, awaiting the rapture, and instead saw the gas station and his car ten feet away. Behind him the short man from the store with the cigarettes was wrestling with the man from the stall, the gun held high. There was a sharp crack as it went off and both men suddenly flew apart like they were being jerked back by bungee cords. They hit the floor and then lay there, respective hands covering their respective heads.

He motioned to them then realised he was beginning to wave. Instead, he ran to the car; found his key and struggled with the seat belt before deciding that the seat belt could wait until he got on to the road.

Fuck, he said, fuck.

He raced towards the highway, jabbing his thumb at the radio. Suddenly the car was filled with music and then a soothing, familiar-sounding voice that no one could fail to find the happiness in. He felt a squeezing in his bladder and then a second of panic at the thought of finding another garage or rest stop and pulling the car over, the thought of having to stop again. Then he noticed the Coke cup rolling around on the seat next to him and he reached for it.

Song 3: Free

The sky was different to how he remembered it, even the times when he was allowed out into the exercise yard. There the light was always bordered by the high prison walls, the heavens made into a rectangle. He was always looking skyward hoping to see it uncontained. That was his idea of freedom: no guards, no fellow inmates, no noise, the air unhindered. He'd served eight years of a twelve-year sentence and as he stood outside the gates in the sunlight – the stone walls and steel mesh fences behind him – he looked up and took it all in until his eyes hurt and his neck ached.

Hey, get out of here, you can't come back in, laughed one of the guards from an observation tower somewhere off to his left. He lowered his head and waved and shouldered his bag, walking towards the bus stop as surefootedly as if he knew where he was going or what he was going to do once he got there.

The station stood at a fork in the road, a low flat-topped building with a seating area and snack machine and matching doors at either end, one facing west, the other east. Visitors to the prison disembarked there and made their way home via there too once visiting time was over. Tired-looking mothers and their sad-eyed children trailed in and out of those doors, loitered on the seats, kicked their feet and waited for a bus door to hiss into life, its gears to grind into place and take them away again. He took a seat in the middle of a bench that looked as though it had been liberated from a church, even down to the bracket at the back where he could imagine finding a small, leather-bound bible. It was quiet; there was no one there from the prison as far he could see. A young couple sat a few spaces down from him arguing in low, intense voices about the next move they should make. He wished he could help; he had no money to give them (the government had given him a meagre handout as they pushed him out of the prison doors) and he knew that was what they needed more than anything else. That and a few more options. He'd once kept moving like they were moving, trying to resist life, hoping that his rootless self could somehow evade consequence, but it almost always came down to places like this – he surveyed the muddied windows that rattled in their frames each time a truck passed by, the empty vending machine, the old magazines, the toilet where the light didn't work and the lock was broken, the locks were always broken. But some winter nights when he'd been on the road, refusing to yield, then places like this had passed for sanctuary; well lit, sheltered and dry — a refuge from the endless night overhead.

I don't want to go back there, said the girl, gathering her jacket around her shoulders, He glanced at them and they both shot him a look back. He quickly averted his gaze and felt the rattle of a truck pulling slowly past. The building vibrating up through his boots and making his ears tingle.

Where else is there? said the young man, we've run out of places to go. The door opened and a woman in a peaked cap walked in, took a black marker pen from a cup next to a large board and started writing down the bus times for the rest of that day. The pen squeaked with each stroke. He saw that there were four buses coming through that afternoon. He looked at the board and determined to take the third one wherever it was going. The young man got up and stood close to the board as if willing the list of destinations to change. He sat next to the girl and said something to her and she shook her head softly and then rested it on his shoulder, pulling her legs up underneath her as she did so. A bus came into view, describing a wide arc and momentarily blotting out the afternoon light with its glass and chrome bulk. It shuddered to a stop and passengers, some he recognised from the visiting hall at the prison, trooped past, their shoulders low, their posture inclined towards the slight hill that led up along the curved road that would eventually take them to the jail and out of sight. One man nodded at him as if in recognition and he knew that he must have passed him as he sat waiting for his father or brother to come and see him. It always took longer than any one of them would have liked to filter through the combination of gates and bag searches before they arrived in the main visitors' hall itself. His brother, without fail, would always ask him what in the hell he was doing in there. It was a signal that he'd already run out of things to say. His father was more reflective and would bring him books and critique them slowly before handing them over. He'd sit there opposite his son with his hand laid flat across the book cover and explain the nuances of the plot, the strengths and flaws of the characters, sometimes even revealing the story's denouement before pausing theatrically and then apologising in a soft voice. Only then would he slide the book across to him. He looked forward to both their visits, though. His brother would reveal sports results as if they were magical tricks he'd pulled from the air. He half expected him to reach over and pull a quarter from behind his ear each time he told him that the Bears had lost.

We get the papers here, he'd say to his brother. We've got a TV room, I see the sports results. But his brother would wave the words away like a cynic dismissing an urban myth and start in with a very literal blow-by-blow account of a title fight he'd seen the previous Saturday night.

Sadly, his brother had got married and moved away which made his visits less frequent the last few years. His father had died two years before when his heart gave out as he was crossing the street three blocks from their home. In the letter his brother had written him afterwards, he told him how his father had reached out and touched the bonnet of a car that had paused to let him pass. The engine idled while his dad had rested there a moment, one hand flat on the bodywork as if it were a book, and then he placed the other palm across his pressed shirt and slid silently to the floor, his head coming to rest against the fender of the car. The car's driver had told the police that he looked like Jimmy Stewart lying there. As he sat in prison reading the letter he was pleased with the analogy, it made him think that his dad's death was peaceful, dignified. His brother had offered to come and get him when he was released, even suggesting he stay while he got back on his feet, but he wanted to roam a little first. He promised to head west to his brother eventually, but for now it was imprecise patterns and hasty plans that he wanted to make.

He'd gone to California as a young man to dream. He vaguely imagined attending film school (waking from sleep, he often saw himself helming a camera, shouting directions attracting admiring glances from his cast and crew), but when he got there, he found that all the women were actresses and all the men potential leads waiting on their break or embittered hacks who only resembled the successful scriptwriters and novelists they emulated in the amount of booze they drank. He was three weeks away from having to give up his tiny apartment at the Villa Elaine when he got a temp job at a suddenly prospering talent agency. He fetched coffee, ran scripts and tapes between departments and offices, manned the front desk and phones and then one day his boss asked him to take an envelope to one of the agency's biggest names. He was the lead in a popular comedy drama that had earnt him a Golden Globe nomination. He lived in an apartment with floor-to-ceiling windows overlooking a fashionable chunk of the Hollywood hills and was in a robe and a pair of shorts when he answered the door. He was charming and his skin glowed as if he'd just stepped off a sunbed or been freshly moulded from plastic; he looked malleable.

Drink? he beamed, walking very quickly towards the kitchen. He'd plucked the envelope from his hands as soon as he'd let him in.

Sure, he said uncertainly as he stood admiring the view of the parched hills and the uncertain white apartment blocks and houses below. Even with the unrelenting air conditioning he could feel the sun through the glass. He looked for the Hollywood sign, but he couldn't see it. The actor returned holding two tall glasses filled with something clear and lots of ice that clinked as he handed it across.

Vodka and tonic, the actor said. That okay?

He nodded and with a gesture the actor invited him to sit. A low glass table with a chessboard sunk into its centre stood between them. The actor opened the envelope and tipped its contents on to the board.

Checkmate, he said and he smiled broadly.

He imagined it was something the actor had said before. The cocaine was compacted from the envelope, but the actor quickly broke it down with a razor blade he'd produced from his pocket. He scooped some up on the corner of the blade and snorted it loudly before offering the blade across and indicating he take some. The actor tipped his head back and sighed happily, then took a long gulp of vodka; he was smiling expectantly, his robe hanging open, he was the kind of brilliant brown you see in imported furniture stores.

He balanced a small crumbling mound of cocaine on the blade and brought it quickly towards his nose before he spilt it. It felt clean and instantaneous as it rushed through him. He looked up at the actor who was holding his drink forward for him to toast. They touched glasses and he said cheers while the actor saluted him with his free hand. Then the actor leant forward and pushed more cocaine on to the blade before inhaling it hungrily, then he dabbed his finger into the powder and rubbed it emphatically on to his gums, poking out his tongue, so his smile looked lopsided.

He didn't go back to the office that afternoon; he didn't go back to the office again. He doubted they'd let him back in if he did. The actor said he liked him, said he could use him, asked him if he needed a job.

I've got this one, he said, but the actor just laughed incredulously. It transpired that the actor didn't just get nominated for Golden Globes, win critical plaudits and ingest cocaine, he moved it around town too. He only dealt to friends and associates, he said, and needed someone to deliver it on his behalf, someone, he said, waving the razor blade around, that wouldn't get into his own stash, someone he could trust. Because, and he emphasised the word, wrapped his lips around it, people trusted him and who was anyone without their reputation, especially in this town.

He stopped and looked around as if only just realising that it was dusk and his apartment was now dark. His head bobbed and his snorting seemed like it was the only sound ricocheting around the hills. He looked up, a white frosting crusted around his nose. It looked like it was glowing in the half-light.

Got a car? the actor asked.

He spent the summer moving from one gated community to another, from isolated hilltop mansions, gleaming and white, to sprawling ranch houses with their own basketball courts and views of the city he'd never seen before. Sometimes, he'd swoop back down into the canyon and feel like he was riding a helicopter over the jutting brows of the hill, LA below, dusty and listless in the daytime, expansive and dreamlike at night. He'd visit the actor three, sometimes four times a week to pick up the supplies and his cash and then he'd work his regular route unless there was a major party or launch happening and then the demand would rise, like people ordering in extra milk over the holidays. The actor would insist that they celebrate their good fortune and thriving business before he set out. A razor loaded with cocaine and a tall glass of vodka and he'd be back out on the sharply inclined streets feeling fresh and alert, always driving too fast for the first twenty minutes or so.

He'd overdone it one night. Sometimes when he'd take a delivery it would be a simple exchange of one envelope for another. Other times he'd be invited in and, much like the first time he met the actor, be asked to hang out, share the cocaine he'd brought and have a drink. It was hard to say no. Firstly, he didn't want to alienate the client (and sometimes it would be a producer or actor he admired) and after the first hit he'd taken at the actor's house he almost always wanted a top-up.

The palatial white house he drove up to was beyond large gates and a grand circular driveway. It was so bright in the sun that it looked burnished. Two huge marble columns stood impassively either side of the heavy twin doors, one of which was ajar revealing a black-and-white checked hallway and a staircase that he could imagine Fred Astaire dancing down. The producer was playing cards with some friends out at the back of the house on a sundeck beneath a large Sol beer umbrella; it looked incongruously cheap given the grandeur of the house. The view, even by the standard of the vistas he'd experienced the last few months, was breathtaking. They were so high up he felt dizzy, the city was like a glistening speck below them, the struts beneath the sundeck the only thing keeping them from falling into the valley below. He swayed slightly and wondered if it was vertigo. The producer shook his hand firmly and asked him to sit. Like the actor he dumped the contents of the envelope onto the table and his friends laughed and cheered. Rolled-up bills were quickly produced and he was invited to dip in with the rest of them. Someone he vaguely recognised from an old TV show he'd watched as a kid handed him a beer and clapped him on the shoulder. Hours later, at the producer's insistence, he was racing down the valley, jumpy at every intersection, back to the actor's house to replenish their supply. The producer had a party that night and now had the creeping fear that the coke he'd ordered wasn't going to be enough.

He worried that he was going too fast and then that to overcompensate that he was going too slow. He checked his rearview mirror assiduously for cops, but it was quiet up here, the only real danger he faced was the sudden curves in the road that encouraged him to race into the sky.

The actor, who was still in his robe, was delighted to see him.

He likes you, he jabbered, wagging a finger at him; I knew the customers would like you, that's why I gave you the job. You're personable, like me. They were both strung out, sniffing heavily and pinching their noses; the actor kept touching his cheek, unsure if the numbness was in his face or fingertips. The drive back up and along the valley wall was like a dream, the cooling air rigid and unresisting as it coursed through the open windows of the car. The producer's house had started to hum with life like he imagined Gatsby's mansion once had and then he remembered that Gatsby was a character in a book and he laughed stupidly.

He came to the next morning in the back seat of his car, his nose was full and there was a grey residue under his nails and on his teeth. He sat up and then lay quickly back down again as his stomach churned and something came loose behind his eyes. He checked his watch and groaned at the time, forced himself to sit up and pulled himself into the front seat. The producer's house stood almost solemnly behind him, both doors now wide open, a lone girl in a sheer-looking cocktail dress sitting cross legged on the rim of the fountain that was the centrepiece at the heart of the circular drive. It had been flowing last night, but was now as still as if the sun had burnt it out. He imagined his racing heart was louder than the radio as he put the car into gear and started to roll slowly down the hill. He reached into the glove compartment and felt about, glancing up occasionally at the road unfurling before him. He found what he had been looking for, an envelope that still had to be delivered later that day. He placed it onto the seat next to him and pulled over, scooped some of the contents onto his nail and quickly thrust it into his nose. His forehead was damp and his hair clung to it, he pushed it back and felt revulsion when he realised how heavily he was sweating. He pulled slowly out into the road and picked his way down the hill, intermittently dabbing at the envelope as he tried to stabilise his equilibrium and stop himself from throwing up. He felt parched. He pulled over at the first store he found and bought a bottle of water which he gulped down at the counter much to the astonishment of the teenage boy who was working there. He must have looked wild. He knew the water was cascading over his chin and chest but his thirst was insatiable. He slammed the plastic bottle onto the counter top with a wide-eyed grin and thanked the boy a little too loudly before he left. He stood outside and noticed the police that were parked across the road from the store. He clambered into his car, keeping one hesitant and fearful eye across the street. He pulled away from the store and ran quite slowly into a car that was coming the other way. He'd forgotten to secure his seat belt and cracked his head sedately, almost methodically, against the windscreen. He sat back with a dazed thud and by the time he'd turned around to the passenger seat there were the policemen looking in through the open window at him, a young officer already had the envelope and its spilt contents in his hands.

He wouldn't give the actor up and so for the first two years of his sentence he found himself in a maximum-security unit in southern California. He refused to meet anyone's eye and did his best to melt into the walls and between the bars when any of the gang members who made up the majority of the prison's population passed him. He ended up sharing a cell with a convicted murderer the other prisoners had christened Cornflakes, though never to his face. That gave him a degree of respect among the other inmates: sharing a cell with a murderer had earnt him points in a scoring system he didn't understand.

I don't know how you can bear it, someone said to him while they were taking their exercise time. The differing gang factions dominated large swathes of the yard, eyeing each other murderously, but those that chose to just exist and stay small tended to congregate at the back wall beneath the two armed observation towers. Very little trouble ever started there. He squinted at the other prisoner; he didn't know what he meant.

Cornflakes, he said, killed his wife and little girl, gutted them both. When the police found him he was squatting naked over the daughter eating cornflakes out of her guts with a spoon. You didn't know? The other prisoner looked at him with incredulity.

Man, we thought you had balls of steel to sleep in a bunk underneath that guy night after night.

Someone like that shouldn't be in here, he said, and he knew his voice was shaking. Shouldn't he be in a psychiatric unit or something? The other prisoner shrugged. Don't knock it, the prisoner said. In one way or another he's looking out for you in here.

And that's how it was until they moved him up to a facility near Chicago twenty-five months later. Its lower security rating was reflected in the prisoners themselves. There were still flare-ups, sudden outbursts of violence, but like him, a lot of the inmates had come from much tougher places and now quietly revelled in the relative calm that none of them wished to shatter.

The second bus had left the station carrying the young couple with it. They'd exited through the door heading east with imploring eyes, hands clutched tightly around one another. He could only wish them well as they paused at the bus door. Then they were sealed in and carried off along a road to who knew where. He checked his watch as the bus driver waved him aboard and took a window seat near the back. He thought he recognised some of the countryside around here, but it had been so long since he'd seen it he could never be sure. He was heading north from Chicago and had no idea about what he might do next, but he had some money in his pocket and knew that even a dingy motel room would seem like luxury after where he'd spent the better part of a decade. The bus pulled into a gas station that doubled up as a convenience store with a large separate washroom out by the back. They could have been anywhere, but he knew they were somewhere outside of Milwaukee, heading away from it he thought. He saw something in the off ramps and the sloping highway to his right that he couldn't discern but he knew. He felt the memories rekindling within him, he remembered being young and driving around with his friends, out of the suburbs and dangerously fast along these roads, smoking cigarettes and worrying their dreams down. I'm going to move out to the coast, he told them a hundred times as the streetlights reflected off their roof and the dark streets passed by in hazy blocks.

He suddenly wanted a cigarette, and even though he hadn't smoked one in years he felt a tingle of excitement and guilt at the idea of unwrapping a pack and tapping it hard on his hand and lighting up, just like he had felt at fifteen. He walked into the store and picked up the first packet he saw, a yellow box of Natural American Spirit cigarettes. There was a man standing by the counter that instantly set him on edge; he was asking the girl serving him for directions. He moved forward and offered him a cigarette.

Where you going? he asked the man and instantly wished he hadn't.

There were men he'd met in prison, dangerous men whom even the guards were wary of. Not just the gang-bangers, but the ones serving the hundred-year jail terms, those to whom time was meaningless because a hundred years may as well be a thousand years and the only certainty in their lives was that eventually they were going to die in their cell. Those men had tortured and raped before finally killing, they were the men who'd killed again once they were inside. The man asking directions was one of those men, he was sure of it. He checked to see if he recognised him from his time in jail, but if it wasn't that, then it was the cruel air he exuded, the bleak, dead centre to him. He wouldn't have been surprised to see the man pull out a gun and shoot the girl behind the counter in the face. The man was impassive, brooding.

West, said the man.

In spite of himself, in spite of the cloud of fear that was expanding in his stomach, he found that he was smiling. His voice started to break.

No you're not, he said, and waited for the man to strike him, but instead he turned on his heel, exited the store and got in his car. He exhaled noisily as the car started to pull away and then felt his stomach tighten again as it pulled in adjacent to the washroom and the driver disappeared inside.

You okay? he asked the girl behind the counter and she nodded, perplexed by his concern. He paid for his cigarettes and walked slowly towards the washroom. The bus he'd travelled in on was idling softly behind him, the bus driver calling all passengers back onboard. He walked back towards the bus, grabbed his bag from the overhead rack and jumped back off, the driver – whose name tag said he was Mal – told him they didn't do refunds.

He walked across the forecourt and past the store and stood close to the washroom door and listened. He could hear the man talking to himself; he sounded like he was holding up his end of a conversation. A loud hey suddenly came through the door and he stepped back in spite of himself, like a boy who had been caught eavesdropping. There was someone else's voice then, he was sure, then the banging of a door and someone was shouting and he charged in.

The scenario surprised him; someone who looked like a latter-day Johnny Cash was barrelling out of the toilet stall, he was shouting and waving a gun around while the man – this vision of evil – cowered in the corner by the open door, his hands over his face. The Cash lookalike was thrusting the gun at him, jabbing the short barrel at his head and shouting incomprehensibly.

You freak, you fucking freak, he kept saying, pushing the gun into the soft flesh at the back of the man's neck.

He got hold of the man and pulled him out of the washroom by the back of his belt and spun him around, causing him to land on his knees in the gravel. The short grey man let out a throaty roar and ran towards him. They collided in the doorway and stood there wrestling for a moment, their hands reaching up for the gun. They came careering out, falling backwards and then the gun went off with a sharp crack and both men threw themselves apart and curled up into terrified huddles on the floor, the weapon suddenly small, still and mute between them.

He looked up and imagined he saw the man waving at him, but then he was gone in a slamming of doors and a squealing of tyres.

CROSS COUNTRY MURDER SONG

He rolled over onto his back and sighed heavily; in the distance he could hear sirens wailing as the patrol cars neared. He wondered how long it would be before he'd see the unbroken sky again.

Chorus

He knew he was driving too fast, but he couldn't bring himself to ease back on the accelerator. He kept attempting to blink the old man in the bathroom stall away, but his face and his gun sat ghoulishly behind his eyelids. He reached under the passenger seat and found his own gun braced there against the metal frame. He looked up just in time to see that he was heading for the side of the road and was being flashed by an oncoming car possibly terrified that a driverless vehicle was headed his way. He pulled the wheel sharply back on course and gave a cheery wave as the other car raced past. Must have thought that was the strangest game of chicken he'd ever seen, said the driver quietly. He was laughing in spite of himself. He checked on the gun again and felt its weight in his palm, admired its shape and drew a thumb slowly across the matt black of the handle. He enjoyed the resistance of the trigger as the safety held.

The first gun he'd seen had been his father's, but he didn't know whose it was when he'd stumbled across it wrapped in a oily rag. Their garden was a giant L framed by trees at the back of the house with an oblong pool set at its corner. In the summer his father would bob along its surface, the swell of his belly breaking the water as he grinned and waved his cigar around, his white legs, dashed with drifting swirls of black hair, the inflatable he lay on buckling with his weight. He'd laugh as the ash broke free of his cigar in dirty rings, floating stubbornly as smoky debris before seesawing slowly to the bottom of the pool. His father's friends would laugh as his mother chastised him for smoking in the water. Hey, he'd say, it's not like I'm going to set something on fire, and he'd cackle, the cigar playing at his lips.

One afternoon he found his father standing silently in the kitchen. It was a Sunday and it was early for him to be back at home.

Want to go for a drive, kid? he asked, staring out at the garden. His mother wasn't home. He had no idea where she might be. Soon they were among the fields, his father gunning the engine as they passed a low red barn with acres of moving green beyond dotted with horses. He could see a boy standing among them, his hand reaching out to the tallest of the horses, his gesture making the animal wary, causing its head to pull back in quick jolts, its curious, beautiful eye regarding the approaching hand with caution. The horse took off with a snap of its mane, its tail suddenly whipping the air. The boy jumped back and the horse came at the fence at a gallop, the three-bar fence acting as a rickety sentry between the road and the farmland beyond. The horse ran its length, keeping pace with their car. His father grinned happily and opened up the engine and the horse harried itself on only feet away and they travelled momentarily neck and neck as if both were reaching to break an imaginary wire. The field divided at its corner and the horse spotted it before they did and threw himself back

63

into the heart of the field, bucking and roiling, his head lolling happily, legs kicking hard as he ran out of sight.

His father hit the driving wheel with his open hand. Hey, he exclaimed, hey!

He grabbed his son's shoulder. Did you see that? he asked, Damn, what a beautiful fucking thing. He looked at him. You don't have to tell your mother I just said that, okay, he said.

You see that horse? his father asked. He nodded. They'd both been made dizzy by the sparks of energy it had given off.

Horses and dogs, I mean the domestic kind, pets, you know, not pack dogs, the wild kind, his father said. He nodded. He did know.

Animals, like that, they just run for fun, his father said. When we run, we're running after something or we're running from it. His father's voice had changed as if he was shifting down a gear like he did when their car approached a bend in the road. His father became quiet. He found a farm driveway he could back up into, turned around and headed back home. He walked up the steps into the house with his arm on the boy's shoulder and then walked into his study and closed the door.

The squirrel was sitting on top of the post, silver grey and alert. It was twitching with life, fidgeting endlessly, shifting its weight around. The family dog, Pascoe, a black Labrador, sat at the bottom of the post patting the earth down with his paws and making a strange low whine that turned into excited yapping. The squirrel clung onto the post and pointed itself at the earth, driving the dog into a frenzy; then it took off with a suicidal-looking leap and darted past the dog and into the thicket of trees that stood at the back of the house.

Shit, he said and raced after the dog as it lurched off in pursuit. Three loping figures in profile frozen for a moment before the squirrel exploded with a burst of speed and hit a tree, running and skipping up its thick trunk and into the higher branches out of sight. Pascoe fared less well and went through a mesh of bracken and bushes, drool gathering at his panting jaws. He chased in after him, calling his name.

Pascoe, suddenly mute, was sniffing around the edges of a dilapidated beehive, a small wooden cube with a sloping roof now discoloured with age. He lifted a leg lazily and added to its patchwork of stains. He pushed the dog back and circled the hive slowly, as if the air might suddenly fill with bees. He touched the panelling on its side and gave himself a start as a piece of wood came loose and hit the floor. Pascoe ran forward barking, his tail making a fan in the air. He shushed the dog and was leaning forward to examine the piece of wood when he saw the tight bundle of oily rags pushed underneath the hive. He pulled it free and was surprised at its weight; he untied it and gasped when he saw the revolver sitting there in his hand. He picked the gun up gingerly and then held it out before him and looked along its barrel. Pascoe whined and backed up behind him. He moved the gun around, aiming the sight at the high branches above him, and then he pulled the trigger. The safety held the trigger in place and without thinking he found the metal nub above the handle and flicked it forward. He pointed the gun at the tiny blossoms of light breaking through the foliage above him and fired. Pascoe ran back towards the safety of the house and he heard the scuttling above him as the higher branches emptied of startled squirrels and birds. Then the housekeeper was racing through the trees followed by his father who he heard before he saw him, his repeated, breathless, Jesus! sounded like a mantra as he came racing across the garden. The housekeeper wrestled the gun from his hand and threw him so violently to one side that he fell. His father came rushing through the brush and clipped the beehive as he did so. His stream of expletives was louder than the gunshot, his *face was red and astonished. He dragged him inside the house and beat him around the face and shoulders until he was doubled up with exhaustion and then he locked him in the basement with a hand towel filled with ice cubes to stem the flow of blood and to help reduce his swollen cheek.*

He'd wanted to kill his father after that, but he knew he was too scared of him. He could only imagine failing, stalling in his actions as he stood over his father's sleeping form and his father coming awake to pull the knife away from him and exact some terrible revenge, his mother's screams in the half-light. He missed his father regardless, he missed him even when he was around, he'd hear him walking about in the rooms above his and his mother was always out of sight, still and watchful in the shadows somewhere. He drifted from room to room in their cavernous house, a figure pinned as a silhouette in the tall windows looking out over the gardens. The kitchen was always full of voices, his father's friends' laughter louder and more prolonged as they stretched into the night.

He slept fitfully in his motel room that night as his father walked his dreams as he once had the upper storeys of his house, silently pacing through room after room but never meeting his son's eye. He was getting ice from the end of the corridor early the next afternoon when he saw the man exiting the room opposite his. As the door opened a woman smiled coyly and placed her hand on the man's forearm and drew him briefly back in, they both laughed and then she let him go and even before she'd fully closed the door he saw the man's face, now turned towards him, change from glassy happiness to gloomy indifference. His look of resignation was almost profound.

The driver waited by his door, listening to the toing and froing outside, the cleaner's cart and the dislocated voices and steps retreating down the hall, and when he heard the woman leave the room opposite his he quickly let himself out and caught up with her at the elevator. He studied her on their descent and then matched her hurried stride across the reception, just beating her to the door that he held open with a flourish. Once they were outside, he asked her about her affair, but he was gentle about it. Her lover's stony face had rattled him and he felt the shadow of his mother's sadness pass over him. She bristled though, no matter his tone, she couldn't understand that he was trying to reach out and help her. He tried to tell her about his father's affairs, about his mother's drinking and how eventually when his mother died how his father had taken to drinking with the same bleak enthusiasm.

Ironic, he said. She was mute though, untrusting. He could see that she wanted to be left alone to unscramble the guilt and lust strangling her thinking. He left her standing in the car park and sat in his car and watched her drive slowly past and away. Her face was rigid with thought and he watched her until she disappeared into the traffic that was pulling onto the highway. He sat for ten minutes while the tears gathered in dark blue blotches on his jeans like ink soaking into blotting paper and then he drove sharply off, cutting across a car that was trying to pull in to the motel. The sound of screeching tyres and someone shouting was all he heard as he pulled away and a headache built behind his eyes.

Song 4: Plastic

The day he came to tell her he couldn't continue the affair, builders were drilling and hammering at the building opposite and she couldn't catch his words. He was gesticulating at her, mouthing his goodbyes, when she grabbed his hand and pulled him into the cool light and quiet of the kitchen where he broke her heart. Even though he was standing very close, she was trying not to listen so that the words would deflect from her and wouldn't count, that they wouldn't have enough weight to drag their relationship down. She stared hard at the pots and pans hanging in an uneven line and tried to address the inverted, ballooning scenario developing in the gleaming reflection of the biggest pot closest to her. She couldn't hear him, but she could see that he was pointing at her and then she realised that he was gone from the pot, from the kitchen and from her.

Her name was Nancy. He was called Kory and he was married to her sister and had been for three years. She hadn't been his first affair, he'd admitted that to her the second time they'd slept together, as she was running a finger through the sweat gathering in the small of his back. She looked across at him and knew it was his way of warning her off, letting her know that this was something that would not last, that he would go back to her sister, just not then (though he was gone within the hour and always would be), but inevitably, ultimately. That's where his life was. He said that so much that it became like a mantra to both of them as if once he left home and came to her that it was in some kind of hinterland, that their actions weren't concrete in this world, that their fucking was without consequence. That there need not be an outcome to this, it was set in time, like a bug caught in amber.

She thought about this as she looked at her bandaged hand. Her thumbs were uneven – or had been – with a bulb of flesh making an imperfect line on her left hand. She'd all but forgotten about it until Kory touched her for the first time (discreetly and at a safe distance from the house) and she'd felt him flinch when his hand had bumped against it. He'd disguised his reaction quickly and smiled as he kept looking from the house to her and told her how he felt about her, how he'd always felt. She wasn't stupid enough to believe him, but she wanted to believe something. Her sister came out of the house and he placed his hand back in his lap and smiled at her again and then he stood up to embrace his approaching wife.

Their affair started soon afterwards. Christmas had passed, but winter still lingered long into the New Year. The snow was still on the ground when she first made love to him; she did wonder later whether it was making love for him too or just fucking. Even later still she'd feel silly and girlish for even allowing herself to ever think that; he was fucking her against the wall of a generic motel room in a building that looked like it had fallen out of the sky and landed near the highway, and in his memory he always would be.

Cosy, she thought to herself as she tried not to think about the orange bedspread or the lifeless-looking carpets as she first entered the room. Dull light played through the window as he produced a bottle of whisky from his bag and went down the corridor to find some ice. She'd enjoyed it and him, though, despite herself. The sex was good and playful, sometimes rough. She found herself smiling as she sat across him and was happy to feel his weight pushing against her as he covered her body with his. She'd had a mole removed from near her mouth next. It was strange to look at herself in the mirror and not see her hand move to it any more, to caress it lightly and wonder what she would look like without it. Now she knew; there was less of her, there was nothing to see, no punctuation to her face any more, she thought, and then wondered what had made her think that.

You look different, her sister said to her, and for a moment she panicked and thought that guilt and satisfaction really could be seen set across someone's face. Your mole, her sister said, and she looked at her again more directly as if trying to balance the two halves of her face: before and after. I liked your mole, her sister said again. Why did you get rid of it? She didn't know, she said, then she said, a mole can indicate cancer, you know. Her sister, a hint of hysteria creeping into her voice leant forward and said in a stage whisper, Your doctor thought you had cancer? She shook her head. No, she said, the doctor never thought that.

They were sitting on high stools at a corner of a bar that neither of them had been to before. There was a silence between them; her sister waved her glass at the barman, ordering another round.

Better to be safe than sorry, right? she said, but her sister just stared at her, at the tiny mark, at the thin line where her mole used to be.

He was pushing his thumb gently into her mouth when he noticed that the mole had disappeared. He traced a finger against the minute scar and held it there a second. The skin was lighter, slightly off. He was still inside her when he asked where it had gone. She told him the lie about the cancer and the doctor's warning, but he seemed impervious to her reasoning. He was staring and seemed not to be listening at all.

I like it, he said, and stroked her face again, pushing himself deeper into her until she gasped happily.

Next she had her lips pumped with collagen. They looked like two tiny pillows. She felt comical and absurd and couldn't wait for them to deflate. Technically, she told herself, this wasn't an operation; this truly was cosmetic, nothing had been taken from her, nothing had been removed. At first she found them freakish and obscenely large, but he had liked them. He couldn't resist nipping gently at them with his teeth, running his lips against hers. She'd stop and regard herself, usually after she'd taken a shower and he had gone, her hair wrapped up in a towel set high on her head. The weight of it toppled slowly backwards, pulling the skin on her face tight. She admired the set of her jaw, the clean line where it met her neck. She pulled down the towel she had draped around her and rearranged her cleavage so her breasts were pushed together, jutting forward, making them both high and round. She pouted at herself and then smiled as the condensation clouded her reflection in the mirror.

The next time they met she'd had her eyelids done: an eyelid lift. It made her eyes feel sluggish and weepy. She'd once had a bad reaction when younger to a cheap perfume and her stinging, perpetually moist eyes reminded her of the insecurity of that time and those teenage years. She hated it. Worse still, he didn't even notice. It had cost more than her lips and didn't even have half the impact. It was late spring by then and her sister invited her to a barbeque in their back yard. She sat in the same seat where months before he'd first touched her and she'd flinched in fear and excitement and he'd recoiled at her imperfect thumb. She willed him to leave the milling group near the kitchen door and to come over and talk to her, but he laughed too loudly with his friends and made pumping actions with his arm as if he were thinking about lofting a football high over the house. Her sister came and sat with her instead, dropping down on to the bench beside her with a sigh.

What are you doing? she asked, staring quizzically into her face as if trying to take all of her in.

About what? she feigned, trying to duck the question. The daylight was broad, the garden glowed almost featureless in the sunshine, and it felt like it was picking out every detail on her upholstered face.

Your mouth, the mole, her sister paused and came in closer for a look, your eyes . . . She sat back as if to focus and made a face that she recognised as her sister concentrating. It was the face she wore when she studied the newspaper or reread a page of a book until the words became less jumbled and conveyed their meaning to her. She was the puzzle and now her sister was trying to solve her. Her sister leant in close enough to kiss her and she sat back startled.

What is going on with you? she asked. Have you met someone new, is this why you're doing this to yourself?

I'm not doing anything, she said, but she avoided herself in mirrors now and never let her fingers trace her face. She missed her mole, she missed the blemish on her skin, she missed the way it felt against the tip of her smallest finger, and how the slight hair on its surface felt when she'd nudged it with her tongue.

She'd had her first lover in her senior year in school and then three more in college. The night she planned to leave the last one he'd got drunk and drove his car off the road, quickly killing himself as he ploughed into the marshy field below. It had nothing to do with her; he'd died without knowing that she was about to leave him. Ignorance too shrouded her friends and family who all gathered quickly around to cluck and moan, keen to let her mourn for a heart long turned cold. She felt guilty about it, but was quietly relieved that she hadn't had to confront him and then let him go out on that road alone with a bottle jammed between the seats and have to think about her as the car slid from under him and left the road. She had a recurring dream after he'd died that she was collecting body parts, limbs and features from different lovers and piecing them together to make herself a new man. In her dream she had slept with enough men to complete her new lover: the right tongue, the perfect eyes, the careful hands (one night she stood there and admired a beating heart pulsing in her palm before she thrust it into the cavern of his chest). She laid all the parts out on a table and watched the flesh right itself, congeal and become whole; he sat up and held out an arm to greet her and then she'd wake up attempting to fathom his features so that she might catch sight of him on the street and run to him and know he was the one.

Sometimes she'd look at her brother-in-law's face in the afterglow, in the muslin-coloured light, and wonder if it was his features drifting in the shadows all those years ago, but she knew better than that. He wasn't here to rescue her; he was only here to save himself.

Once, after he'd left the motel, she'd showered slowly and surprised herself by crying under the hot jets of water. She had no idea who or what she was crying for, she felt no regret and no guilt that she was conducting an affair with her sister's husband. She did however feel herself fading with every encounter, with every heated embrace squeezing just a little more air from her until her lungs felt permeable, her skin too translucent and thin. She stood in the elevator and thrust out a hand as someone called and asked her to hold the door. The man held her gaze as he entered the lift, thanking her with a nod. They rode down the three floors in silence and he crossed the foyer with her, matching her step for step. The receptionist smiled at her as she passed and the man stepped ahead of her to hold the door open.

They know you here, he said, indicating the receptionist. She was surprised to hear him speak.

I think he was just being polite, she said, wishing her voice was more forthright, more emphatic. He smiled as she said it; he was walking across the parking lot with her now. The highway was feet away behind a tall hedge; she could hear cars swishing past. She'd only been inside a matter of hours, but couldn't quite place where she'd parked her car.

My father used to have affairs, he said, all the time. It just about broke my mother's heart. He looked at her evenly.

I'm guessing your guy has a family, he said, but without rancour or malice.

I don't think it's any of your business, she said and was sorry the instant she said it.

It isn't, he agreed. I don't know what my father got out of it. He was a powerful man: I can't imagine it was self-esteem. What about you, what about your man?

She spotted her car and made towards it. He did nothing to stop her.

My mother, he said, and in spite of herself she slowed down to hear what he had to say. She turned to look at him.

She, my mother, he said, read somewhere that emotion is stored in the liver. Did you ever read that? She nodded, it sounded familiar. He'd stopped and was leaning back on a car that she was sure wasn't his. He didn't look like he'd care if his shifting weight set an alarm off.

There's a theory, he continued, that alcoholics are trying to destroy the liver to dull their feelings, to kill the pain there, you know? She didn't, but she nodded all the same.

My mother took this to heart, the longer my father stayed away, the more she drank. He paused and drummed the fingers of both hands against the bodywork of the car. It was cancer that killed her, he said, but the drink played its part. Softened her up for the disease, if you see what I mean?

She was very still though she felt like she was trembling. She said nothing.

The funny thing is, he continued, my dad died two years later pretty much of a broken heart. When my mother was around he couldn't be at home, but when she was gone he couldn't be anywhere else. He used to wander from room to room in our house as if he might happen upon her somewhere, in one of the bedrooms squaring things away, you know? Some animals do that, search for their dead mates after they've gone. They mourn them. My dad did that, he kept moving from room to room; I'd hear him from the floors below shrieking and calling, his booming voice filling the stairwells and then when he'd exhausted all the rooms, when he'd finally quietened down, he sat in his chair and he drank to take the pain away too. Those were my last memories of him, sitting in that chair, getting steadily smaller and inviting me to sit down and take a drink with him. He was an alright guy, he had his problems too. We all do.

She nodded, but was still mute.

I have to get moving, he said. He smiled and tipped his head and then he was striding purposefully through the parking lot towards the exit gate. She sat in her car momentarily dazed. Then she pulled the mirror down towards her and sat looking into her own eyes. It was no one she knew.

She'd tried liposuction by the autumn and had some work done on the bridge of her nose too. He'd complained about the small scar the tube they'd carried her fat through had made at the base of her stomach and at the top of her thighs. She looked at the loose fat gathering below his chin as he quietly complained and thought very hard about leaning forward and tweaking it as he talked. Instead she lay back on the bed and wondered how long she could make love on an orange bedspread. He'd gone before winter, leaving her in the kitchen of her sister's home as builders worked on an extension on their neighbours' house. She'd wanted it to end, but the ending felt abrupt and sharp and after the door had closed she felt wretched and couldn't stave off the hollow feeling spreading inside of her. It went to her fingertips and she had to shake her hands to get the feeling back. Her sister walked in and told her how she couldn't stand the noise coming from next door any more and then she placed her hand on her wrist and asked her if she'd been crying.

It had been over a year since the affair ended. Her sister had never found out about them, but had often hinted that she thought Kory was having an affair with someone he worked with. She made agreeable and sympathetic noises and thought about him out at a motel on the interstate somewhere looking for flaws in the next naked body. Her sister stared intently at her profile. She used her finger to move the ice around in the tall glass she was drinking from and then took a long pull at it until it was empty.

Are you done having work? her sister asked her.

I don't know if you ever know – she had taken to quoting her surgeon for conversations like this – time waits for no man, she said, and she smiled and enjoyed the feeling of the skin constricting around her eyes. Her face was taut; she imagined drumskins pulled tight as she let her fingers idle around her mouth and throat.

Have we got time for another one? she asked, but her sister shook her head, no. She had to pick her daughter up and so they drove together to the shopping mall, where, she thought, she could probably get a drink while they waited. She found a seat at a bar that looked down into a cross-section of shops, each floor linked by endlessly revolving escalators carrying shoppers from floor to floor. She waved the barman over and ordered another drink and waited for her sister and niece to return.

She recognised her former workmate almost instantly, though she could tell by the body language of the woman approaching her that she wasn't so sure.

Nancy, she said, but the word went up at the end and the question hovered above the bar between them.

She stood to embrace the woman and felt for her thickening back beneath her hands. She pulled back to look into her eyes again and all she saw were the crow's feet and the lines around her mouth and the small sack of fat suspended beneath her chin.

You look so well, she cooed, and they held each other again and as she pressed her head into her friend's shoulder she caught sight of herself in a column of mirrors opposite. Her reflected skin gleamed and as she smiled at herself she thought, happily, of a grinning skull. She turned her head and thought she saw a blemish, but decided it was light and the poor quality of the shopping-mall mirrors. She relaxed and pulled herself away. They stood opposite each other, their hands linked.

Tell me, she said. Have you got time for a drink?

Chorus

The basement was tall and wide, but there were no windows and so no natural light and as soon as he'd entered and found himself standing on the platform that led to the stairs down he felt ill at ease. He recognised faces from his precinct and one of the ambulance crew too; they were easing a limp body from one of the wooden boxes — they looked like coffins from where he stood. There was a body bag, zipped and containing something slight, as if the remains had settled at the bottom; it lay nearby waiting to be dispatched. He walked back out into the high-ceilinged hallway, savouring the air and the light and over to the policewoman who was comforting the housekeeper. She was doubled over with her hands covering her face. She was weeping so much that her torso was convulsing; it looked like she was going into shock.

Detective Moon, the policewoman said as he approached. She had her hand on the housekeeper's trembling back. She gave him a note and he moved into the sunshine flooding in through the tall windows at the back of the house to read it. It was simple enough. Mona, it read, here are the keys to the basement and the boxes I keep there. Please open them and let my friends out. Give me a day before you call anyone. Thank you for everything. And then at the bottom his signature. The policewoman handed the detective the keys that had come with the note, the fob was a small, circular plastic frame holding a picture of a young boy with his arms around a Labrador, it looked as though they were both smiling.

This him, Mona? the detective asked the housekeeper and she looked up at him and nodded.

Did you give him a day before you called anyone? he asked her and she shook her head and began to cry again. Do you want to tell me about it? he asked and pulled up a chair next to her. He handed her a tissue he'd fished out of the packet in his pocket. People were always in tears on this job, he thought.

You found the note this morning, he asked, along with the keys? She nodded and sat up as if the act itself would stop her shaking.

I get here about ten, she said, her eyes worried with tears; she placed the tissue in her lap and held the sides of her chair tightly as if the room were about to tip. Sometimes he'd be here, she said, sometimes not. I'm used to the notes, they usually ask for more towels, that he needed the car cleaned, that sort of thing, you know.

I get the idea, the detective said.

So when I saw the note — she looked at the note now as if it had given her a paper cut — I wasn't sure what to do. She began to shake again, her chest heaving with sadness and grief. I don't usually go into the basement. It's always locked, she said.

Never curious? asked the detective, which raised a smile.

One less room to clean, she said and for a moment they looked as though they'd forgotten about the bodies lying below them.

Mona took the bunch of keys from where they lay, bunched like a dormant spider on the table near the window. She read the note three times and it still made no sense. At first she thought that maybe he'd been keeping rabbits down there, but then why wouldn't he have just housed them near the back in a hutch and given them some light? More than this, she thought he might suddenly appear in the hallway laughing that maniacal laugh of his and grab her by the shoulder and explain the joke in his usual breathless way. She noticed that the garage was open though and one of the cars, the black one, was gone. She took the keys, approached the heavy door to the cellar and jiggled the heavy padlock until the bolt turned in her hand.

The size of the cellar surprised her, the thick darkness barely illuminated by the light coming in behind her. She reached out and found the rail and gripped it tightly in order to quell the sickly fear that she felt moving around in her stomach. Then she heard the low moan coming from somewhere beneath her feet and quickly stepped back into the hall, the sound of her heart filling her head, the cool light of the hallway suddenly a sanctuary as she felt the sun on her shoulders. She peered once again into the darkness and imagined a hand reaching out to her and pulling her in. She stood swaying for a moment and stepped forward with the keys clenched in her fist ready to strike out at the figures she imagined waiting for her. She took the first step slowly, felt around for the light switch and held her breath as the oblongs and squares of light buzzed into life overhead. No one came screaming at her, but she still couldn't bring her heart down to a manageable rate. It thudded rapidly as she slowly took the stairs. She'd spotted the boxes draped with chains to her right as soon *as the light had come on, but couldn't bring herself to look directly at them. She kept them in her peripheral vision as she descended into the basement, convinced that one of the lids was about to spring open and reveal a spectre from her childhood dreams. There was another low moan and it took everything for her not to vault the stairs and leave the house running. The skin on her neck was suddenly raw and cold and she realised her hands were shaking. She forced herself to read the note again and take whatever solace she could find in the word friends that was written there. She traced her finger over it and called out.*

It's okay, I'm here to help, I'll get you out. The boxes were indifferent and still and for a moment she was terrified that the moaning hadn't come from the boxes at all, but from somewhere else in the cellar, that someone lay waiting underneath the stairs she was standing on, furtive and predatory and the note had been their way of enticing her down here in order to trap her. She didn't want to end up in a box, craning to see the light through the thin hole punched in its lid. She felt trapped then and imagined never being able to stretch out her arms or work her legs, but to be tethered to the spot, held in place, eventually lowered into the ground, her cries ignored as the earth took her away. She shook the thoughts from her head and tried to focus on the boxes before her. The smell was damp and deep, almost fungal. There were thin, glittering pipes of burnt yellow leading from the boxes to a tall glass bottle near the bottom of the stairs. Another bottle with a feeding tube at its end stood on a low table nearby. There were six boxes in all, set in a circle around an upturned crate. Three were open and empty, their lids hanging back listlessly on their hinges; one was closed though chains hung freely from its side and two were locked shut, bound tightly, the steel links making snug circles around the wood. She approached the first box and flipped back the lid and then stepped quickly back. The lid clattered open and the noise made her recoil, her hand moving to protect her face. It was empty, but it smelled fresh and rank as if something had slithered away just before she'd got there. She checked the shadows beneath the stairs expecting to see eyes peering back at her, but it was quiet and still except for the low hum of the lights overhead. She wrestled with the padlock on the first box until the lock clicked free and she pushed the chains away until gravity took hold and they uncurled themselves from the box in speeding, rattling lengths, settling on the floor in a heavy coil. Recognising there was someone inside, she opened the lid more slowly, but took an instinctive step back as two bluebottles rose in buzzing circles. The girl was pale and small; her feet didn't even reach the bottom of the box. She was still and quite dead, her hands drawn up into two tiny fists as if she'd tried to resist the oncoming night by sheer force of will. Mona tried to see where the bluebottles had risen from and then one appeared crawling slowly from the pocket on the short jacket she was wearing. She reached forward and lifted the flap to find a slowly seething ball of them attached to what must have once been an apple. She snapped her hand back and shook it violently until the bluebottle that had attached itself to her hand flew free. She was shaking as she approached the last box. The moaning had stopped and she was scared that she'd find another dead body. Each time she closed her eyes she saw the young woman's clenched fists beating at the lid of the coffin, her screams the only sound in the encroaching darkness. She worked the padlock and pulled the chains free with a gasp and then gently eased the lid back. The man lying there was as still as the girl, and she felt the disappointment rising in her chest and began to chastise herself for hesitating, frozen to the spot on the stairs. Then he let out a low moan again and she moved quickly forward and grabbed his hand, his fingers clutching feebly around hers. He opened his eyes slowly and then closed *them again as the light struck him full in the face. Sensing his anguish, she stood over him and cast her shadow across him to shield his eyes.*

Hold on, she said, hold on, and gently closed the lid again. Then she ran, still talking to him or to herself, she didn't know. I'll get help, I'll get help, hold on, she said as she took the stairs two at a time.

Detective Moon made his way back down the stairs to the basement as the paramedics carried someone on a stretcher, still alive though barely, up to the ground floor.

Detective, said a patrolman he knew but couldn't name. He nodded. The only survivor? he asked, indicating the man on the stretcher as he disappeared through the open door.

Yep, said the patrolman. The girl in the other box was already dead and it looks as though someone had been in the third one until recently. It still smells pretty lively.

He looked in at the boxes, there were holes in the bottom of each with catheters running through them, the lids had scratch marks on the inside. They smelt of decay and fear and blood and piss. The house, or its inhabitants at least, were well known to the police throughout the state, but everything had gone quiet here since the father of the family had died.

The kid wasn't involved in any of his dad's business, as far as we knew, he said and the patrolman nodded, though he didn't know if that were true or not.

What's missing? he asked.

A body, said the patrolman, looking in at the empty box. The other three don't look as though they've been used for a while and a car's gone from one of the garages. The rest of the guys are checking upstairs now.

The note wasn't giving anything away, the detective said. Did the

*guy in the box say anything? As he asked, the paramedics returned
and lifted the body bag onto the stretcher and carried it away. It offered
little resistance.*

Who's in there? the detective asked them.

*Some girl, said the first paramedic, looks young, looks like a runaway,
there were tracks on her arm, but it's hard to tell. There's not much
left of her.*

Not much left of her, the detective repeated. What, like remains?

*Not like that, like she went down to nothing, said the paramedic,
like she gave in. And he nodded and found himself writing this down
as the paramedic said it.*

*He went back up the stairs where Mona told him that it was the
black Lexus that had gone from the garage; it had always been his
favourite car.*

*Does he own a gun? the detective asked. Lots of guns, she replied
and then told him how he would spend his days down at the periph-
eries of the property setting up targets on his makeshift range. Some
days, she said, all you heard from morning until night was the sound
of gunfire.*

*He sighed. Can you show me where? He followed her down through
the expansive garden to the high hedges and trees that bordered the
carefully kept lawn. There was a small, weathered cross stuck in the
ground across from the path they were on. It listed badly.*

Pet? he asked her.

*The dog in the photograph, she said, and pushed past the bushes
and on into the trees. In the clearing there were the remains of a
beehive with a flat piece of wood balanced on the top acting as a
makeshift table. The clearing had been pared back to give the makeshift
shooting gallery some range. There were various targets, some charging
silhouettes, others conventional numbered circles, pockmarked with bullet*

holes. When he saw the figure propped up against the trunk of a fallen tree he drew his gun and motioned for the housekeeper to step back. He moved slowly forward, but knew before he was within ten feet that it was from the third box. He moved to check the pulse at his neck and then he saw the black holes grouped closely on his chest. Pieces of a paper target were still stuck to him, held in place with congealed blood.

What is it? asked the housekeeper, but she kept her distance.

Target practice, I guess, said the detective. And then he shepherded the housekeeper from the clearing, through the sun-filled trees and back to the house where he knew he'd be able to find some help.

Song 5: Box (Reprise)

His office ceiling was low, but the room stretched on forever. There were thousands of lightbulbs of differing shapes and sizes that covered most of the available space above his head. Some were burnt out and black, others hypnotically bright, one or two flickered indifferently, buzzing into darkness and then blooming back into silent life. The light didn't reach much past the bulbs themselves, penetrating no more than two or three feet down from the ceiling and barely dispersing the creeping gloom. The room was filled with binders and boxes full of files and filing cards. Some bulged with paper, precariously stacked, but somehow they remained intact. There was no obvious attempt at order. Red, black and green folders dominated in the main, but the odd boxy oblong of navy blue or steely grey stuck out (literally in some instances) here and there. In the distance, when a heavy door banged open and shut, the discordant tapping of hundreds of typewriters could be heard clicking away, tiny metal keys striking red and black ribbons, the inky cloth deadening the impact. Like an army marching in its socks, he thought. Endless tiny silver bells resonating shrilly and abruptly, then the sudden zipping sound as rollers were pushed from right to left and a new sentence began to run from one margin to the other, a still faintly vibrating bell waiting to come pealing into life again. He preferred it when the door was closed; the sound hurt his head otherwise. He looked up as someone came in to load another pile of black filing boxes on to the edge of his desk. He gave the courier a baleful look, but they'd already turned their back and squared their shoulders and were soon lost among the teetering columns of paperwork. He heard the door opening and the trilling metallic chorus rose up again in a rush until it was muffled by the heavy wooden door slamming shut. Then it was suddenly quiet. He stood up and walked to the window, but the window was always dark, the view always obscured. He peered at the glass, but the only thing he saw was himself looking back. His brow, he noticed, was furrowed. He rubbed hard at the jutting shelf of flesh between his eyes. He looked tired, dissatisfied. Another bell rang somewhere, not a typewriter bell, something with more clarity. He turned to see an envelope set squarely on his desk and crossed the room to open it. The index card inside was covered in tight red script and in one corner there was a small box that someone had neatly ticked. He held it up and regarded it over the top of his glasses, then he walked to the first pile of black folders and carefully pulled the top box down from the unsteady pile. Inside the box there were hundreds of index cards tightly bound together in neat batches. He pulled the elastic bands apart and playfully catapulted one in a looping arc into the corner of the office. It bounced off a red folder and disappeared into a shadowy corner. He matched the card from the folder with the one in his hand, found a paperclip in his top pocket and joined them together, making sure their corners were precisely matched. He placed them in the folder and then returned the box to its jaggedly concave pile. He grunted a little as he pushed it back into place and then he returned to his desk and waited. He'd filed him away, which meant that he'd be here soon.

He woke in darkness and lay there letting his eyes adjust. It was quiet, just the low hum of an air conditioning unit and the occasional flickering in the shadows that made him think someone was coming, but he was alone. The box he was in was shut tight with a slit in the hinged door set almost directly above his face that let the air in. He had kicked and thrashed around in the tight blackness when he'd first awoken, but he'd simply bloodied his knuckles and cracked his knees, the impact making him exhale loudly. That had been how long ago, hours or days? He didn't know. The space was too confined for him to even raise his watch to his face; he was immobile, held, stilled. A figure finally approached the box after moving slowly about in the darkness above and flicked a switch that filled the basement with shocking white light. It was as if the walls had been broken down and daylight allowed to come flooding through the room. He blinked rapidly, tears flushing across both cheeks, and found himself gulping hard as if his head had been thrust underwater, then allowed briefly back to break the surface before it came rushing once more into his mouth. His coughing racked his chest and the voice shushed him. Lying there in the dark he could hear keys jangling against a hip, he heard a bottle of wine being slid from a shelf, the chink of glass as it was manoeuvred free, he waited for someone to speak, but the footsteps faded, disappearing up a set a wooden stairs. There was a pause and the darkness suddenly shrouded him again as a door locking shut was the only hook he could find to attach his fear to. At first he worried about things rushing up at him, tearing the box apart, lunging hungrily. Then some days he'd pray for something to break the box and make him free, if only momentarily.

He'd been attacked while sleeping in the park before and so when the man had approached him on the secluded bench he was instantly wary, but he'd proffered beer and money almost instantly and so then he thought that he was simply cruising the park to hit on him. Some guys came out here, on a temporary lam from their real lives, and offered to suck his cock for cash. He knew guys who did it, and even though he'd lost himself somewhere, he hoped he still retained his dignity. He couldn't square those actions away no matter how hungry or thirsty he got. The man had just laughed when he'd told him this.

I'm not that guy, he'd said to the man, attempting to hand the crumpled dollars back to him. He'd held onto the beer, though. It was cold and felt right in his fist.

I'm just out here helping my fellow man, said the man and he smiled as he said it. It was dusk and only getting darker.

What happens, asked the man, to put a man like you out

here amongst all this? He indicated the neat verges and lush flowering islands of the surrounding park landscape. He patted the bench they were seated on.

Aren't there places you can go at night, shelters, hostels?

He was chugging the beer and only half-listening. The dollar bills sat between them and he was thinking of the places he'd slept in the last few months, the basements, the benches, the hallways of boarding houses, next to a heating duct out by the airport, the foyers of banks where they kept their teller machines, underneath bridges, in store doorways. He'd spent the occasional night in shelters, but there was always fighting and noise there and noise was the one thing he couldn't stand. The man was staring at him and when he turned to look at him he saw his mouth twitching as if he couldn't control his emotions, as if he couldn't, as his dad used to say, keep a lid on things.

I'm sorry, he began. He knew that he'd missed something, something that this stranger seated next to him thought important and now he was angry that he'd missed it. He could always sense fury and misery on people as if they were telegraphing their thoughts, their actions as obvious as those of feral dogs. The twitch of the lips, he knew, was one step away from a widely swung fist, a lunging head. He'd been in enough bars, in enough bar-fights, to become alive to the ions of energy in the smoky air as they crackled with the looming threat of impending violence. Now out here in the early autumn night he felt the irresistible twist and a turning of things, of an animal readying itself for attack. He hunched in on himself ready to take the blow and judged the weight of the can in his hand to see if it had enough heft to it that he might use it as a weapon. He tried to stem the charged current rising in the air around him, the bloody sparks of the inevitable blow, but the man was staring at him silently now, his reddened eyes unblinking in his thin, pale face. Then there was a sound behind him and two other men moved quickly forward from beneath the bushes and trees, clamping a gloved hand (he could smell the leather invading his nostrils) over his mouth and pinning him against the bench. One embraced his while the other held his head in place from behind as the man drew a hypodermic syringe from his coat pocket and placed the point gently into his neck and pushed the plunger home. From a distance they made a strange tableau: the four men in an embrace, three of them looking almost tenderly on at their fallen friend. The men carried the unconscious figure into the shadows and then one picked up the crumpled bills from the bench and took a drink from the beer can, wiped his mouth and threw it on to the grass where its contents oozed into the earth leaving a fleeting golden trail that bubbled into nothing. Moments later it was quiet and the next person that came along merely picked up the can and placed it in the bin.

Hey! He shouted, Hey!

He pummelled at the lid of the box, he kicked against the wood until he felt a sudden tugging in his crotch. He calmed suddenly and brought his hands into his lap, his knuckles brushing against the wood pressing down on him. There was a catheter running down the inside of his thigh, taped to his leg, disappearing out of the bottom of the box. The sense of intrusion made him moan loudly and his voice was echoed somewhere off to his right. Someone was nearby, their desperation intermingling with his. He stopped, terrified by the sounds. When he was younger his mother had taken him to her Pentecostal church where almost every service ended with the congregation speaking in tongues, a swaying mass praising The Lord, hands raised high before passing out with their mouths open, unquestioning like salmon stranded on a rock. It scared him and he'd stand very close to his mother, his hands clenched tightly as he clung to her skirt, hiding his face as people gesticulated and fell all around him. He bit his lip and waited for the moaning to stop and was surprised when it slowly became a soft tuneless humming, like the sound of a distracted child amusing itself. He called out, but was ignored as the noise became softer and more enchanted. The lights overhead buzzed into life and the steps approached quickly and he felt someone hovering over his box. A tube appeared through the slit and he instinctively nuzzled at it like a lamb, but he couldn't remember how he knew to do this, had he done this before? He licked indulgently at the nozzle and felt instantly calmer, almost dreamlike. A hand came through the slit and stroked his cheek and he welcomed the touch.

You're settling in, good, someone said and then he felt himself fading into a dreamless sleep.

Whenever he woke he imagined that he was undergoing a CT scan and that the humming he heard was the gently revolving drum dissecting the inner workings of his brain and feeding the information in hazy blue sheets to the rows of doctors seated behind the glass just out of sight. Then he'd smell the wood and the oil of the box, the musty, still air. Once, he'd been blinded by the light overhead – the difference between his enforced night and day was becoming more extreme as he grew more weary and his muscles became more atrophied – and listened fascinated as the box nearest his was opened and the person lying listlessly there was removed.

Is he the one who sings? he asked in a voice that he didn't recognise as his own. A shadow moved across his box and he saw a silhouette briefly take shape and then shatter in the light.

Sang, said the figure, correcting him. He hefted the small, lifeless form over his shoulder and carried it away.

He played that scenario over and over in his head; it was the new hook he hung his thoughts and fear on. He became aware of his own inertia, of the liquid going into and out of his body, that he was just a vessel transporting fluid from one point to the next. I'm an aqueduct, he thought, and smiled in spite of himself. He could barely feel his face any more; he was becoming as lifeless as a mannequin, adrift in the void. He'd try to talk to the man when he came to see him. He could sense his presence, feel him sitting there on an upturned crate sometimes with the lights on, sometimes in the darkness. The man reached out and touched the boxes with the flat of his hand and would talk in a low voice. He sounded distracted and sad and would never engage in conversation directly. As he lay in the box he'd call out to him with words that sounded as soft as tissue paper, but the man would just shush him and again the slow blackness would descend and when he came to again the cellar would be empty and still.

As he drifted between consciousness and unconsciousness he discovered a place where his mother and her friends gathered to pray and worship; a tall building, brightly lit, so much so that the windows' golden glare made him want to shield his weakening eyes. There was always something in the far corner of the room though; a wooden box set on legs that the light never seemed to reach. His mother was talking to him, holding on to his hand, but he couldn't resist the coffin-shaped box at the end of the room. One night he found himself standing there listening to the whimpering, and he leant forward trying to make out the features of those inside, but the thin slit on the lid made it impossible to see and every time he leant forward his shadow rushed in and filled the space like sand. He tried the lid, but the heavy chains wrapped around it and the hefty padlock meant it couldn't be prised open. He hadn't seen the man before then, he hadn't noticed him among the congregation, never seen him as one of his mother's friends, but he was the first person that offered to help him. He was tall and broad, his shirtsleeves rolled up, he noticed the ink on his fingers as if he'd recently been poring over a ledger. He wore a pair of rimless oval spectacles that he kept perched on his head and he kept rubbing at the space between his eyebrows as if his sinuses or stress were a constant source of trouble.

We could get him out of there, if you wanted to, was the first thing he said to him, a giant hand placed on his shoulder. The wailing of his mother and her friends rose in a thick rope of voices that stretched to the ceiling.

But the chains, he said indicating the thick swathe of black links held tightly around the box, wrapped like a python squeezing the life out of its prey. The tall man leant forward and placed his hand on the steel links and they fell apart and dropped to the floor. The tall man stepped back and invited him to open the lid and look inside and as he did so the light burst through the room and burnt itself into every corner, silencing the voices and leaving only the glowing sun outside to make shapes through the tall windows, the promise of another day to come.

He was back inside the box, but he could feel the tall man standing over him.

I can get you out of there, the tall man said. But it will cost you everything you have.

I don't have anything, he said.

Then, said the tall man, we have a deal.

There were voices then, a clamour at the top of the stairs, a woman's voice louder than the rest; he could hear keys, heavy footsteps coming quickly towards him. The lights were on and someone was calling, his box was being jostled, he heard a padlock snap open and the sound of chains falling to the floor. There was a woman standing over him, she placed her hand in his and then she was gone again and when she returned there were men with her, one of them tried to help him sit up and as he did so he felt nauseous and light-headed. He felt himself being carried up the stairs and into a brilliantly lit hallway, but he was too weak to raise an arm and shield his eyes.

He made the papers and the TV news, the grisly details of the story fascinated the public and he found himself as something of a minor celebrity. His dazed, inquisitive face looked back at him in a glare of flashbulbs from front pages. The nurses would bring them in and sit with him as he read his own story. He'd catch them staring at him sometimes trying to gauge what he couldn't guess. When he finally managed to regain the use of his legs and left hospital a small crowd of well-wishers had gathered outside to cheer him as he left. He'd been in the box for almost a month. He'd told the police and doctors that it had felt like days. The man had fled, they said, taken his car and vanished, left a note for the maid telling her where to find the boxes, the FBI were looking for him now.

What about the tall man, he asked the police officer, didn't he call you? The policeman looked perplexed, he scanned his notes, he didn't know anything about a tall man he said.

His brief notoriety brought him money and even job offers and for a while he found himself living in one of the large houses set in their own grounds that overlooked the city. His benefactor had offered him free room and board for as long as he needed. Even though he was left alone most of the time he felt beholden to him and consequently he felt trapped. Sometimes at night, the benefactor would come to his room and try to engage him in conversation, ask him what had happened to him, talk to him about his time in the box. Afterwards he would dream he was back there in the cellar with the soft voice sounding in the darkness next to him. He'd wake with a start and short of breath and then walk through to the kitchen and out of the back door and stand in the land-scaped gardens looking down at the distant city. One night he kept on walking and let himself out through a wooden gate set in the high stone wall and disappeared down the hill without once looking back.

Within weeks he was back sleeping on a park bench. Even though strangers made him skittish, he felt more comfortable out in the world. He was sleeping on a bench when he woke to feel someone going through his pockets; he came to with a start and grabbed at the thief's wrist. With his free hand the thief lunged at him with the kitchen knife he was holding. He saw the wooden handle and the dull blade as the knife snagged at his neck and cut into his throat. He slumped back and gasped as the thief panicked and ran. They found him the next morning, his blood black and pooled beneath the bench, his head listing at a strange angle. He made the papers again, his sad, strange story giving commuters pause, the benefactor paid for his funeral and they buried him on the hill near the house where he walked from that day to go meet his fate.

He was standing in an office, the sound of typing coming through the door. As he stood there a lightbulb slowly lit up above his head. In the distance, beyond the boxes and boxes of files, someone was seated at a desk. He motioned to him and as he approached him he recognised the tall man, his glasses perched low on his nose. He peered up at him over the lenses and indicated he sit in the seat in front of him. There was a folder open on his desk and he was staring intently at a white oblong card. He turned it over so that it was face up, the infinitesimally small script was hard to read in the hazy light. He reached forward and took the card, but could only make out the ticked box and an acronym: IOU. The tall man reached forward and held his wrist and he found himself thinking about his mother and her friends and realised how very far away they were. Then for an instant it got darker and he looked up at the endless blanket of flickering lightbulbs but he knew he'd find no comfort there.

Chorus

The driver stepped inside of the Motel 6 and steeled himself for the curious glance of the hotel clerk. He'd become used to the unflinching stare as his appearance became more dishevelled. He'd once surprised himself stepping into an elevator, as the doors parted and the full-length mirror stood before him to reveal the bearded, wide-eyed stranger with the mussed hair and streaks of oil and dirt on his shirt. He gasped audibly and tried to pat down his hair on the short journey to his room. Later as he spent more time in his car and less at hotels and motels, his urge to keep moving became more fevered, he felt paranoid in those rooms, checking the wardrobes, darting quickly into the bathrooms, pulling back shower curtains. Ultimately, his appearance began to deteriorate, the stubble a little longer, the eyes a little wilder, the headaches a little stronger.

Fucking Alice Cooper, he would later mumble to his reflection, as his hair grew greasy and lank, the rings around his eyes ever more troubled and dark. His journey, increasingly disjointed and frenetic, saw him, unknowingly, often, doubling back. He'd come close to running short of gas and struggled to work out where he'd been. He'd lost track of the maps he'd balled up and thrown from the car in anger and frustration. He once returned to a roadside gas station three hours after he'd already been there. When he sauntered in to pay for his petrol and pick up some snacks, the teenage boy behind the counter greeted him with a mix of courtesy and surprise.

Get lost? asked the boy, returning his change.

Nope, said the driver, just heading west. He adopted the stance of a surfer on his board indicating with an outstretched arm – as if for balance – what he assumed was true west.

Need a map? asked the boy for the second time that day, uncertainty creeping into his voice.

You don't need a map when you're on an adventure, the driver said, happily not recognising the person who had served him only hours earlier.

I guess not, said the boy watching his thin frame exit the store and make for his car.

Sometimes as he drove he listened to the CD player, more often to the radio. Talk shows, Classic Rock stations, sports networks with double header hosts who punctuated their discussions (one would assume one point, the other the exact counterpoint, the subject matter was almost secondary) by bashing a miniature gong as an exultant full stop to their yammering. The babbling and righteous, the laconic and insipid, all human life, he thought wearily, is here. Call-in hosts with an agenda to bait the listener (which must have worked on more than one occasion when he found himself leaning forward in his seat to scream at the radio) and rouse the audience to interaction. It didn't take much, listeners sounded like they were queuing up to play punchbag to the braying hosts. Some songs would take him back to his basement. He used to play music for his friends in their wooden boxes, sometimes to soothe them, sometimes himself, sometimes just to drown out the moans and pleas.

As he became more reliant on the interior of his car and less sure of the outside world he found ways not to leave the safe confines of his vehicle. He amassed a collection of containers to piss in as he travelled. Sometimes when his confidence was high, he arranged the receptacle while negotiating the road in front of him, cheerily placing himself in position while overtaking and occasionally tuning in the radio dial. He tried a range of cups and containers in a series of trial and error that really was hit and miss.

Things he pissed into as he drove included a Coke cup, a Gatorade bottle, a Pepsi Big Gulp cup (and what a gulp, it took him three attempts to fill it), a Burger King container (with appallingly splattered results. He might as well have lain his dick on his thigh and let go. It was far more porous than he thought too; it had stained the car seat before he'd notice the box seeping). A KFC bucket, it made a deep, drumming sound he found very satisfying, he played with the flow, stemming the rope of piss, building up the pressure and letting it go again with a rattling splash. The Colonel's cheery face vibrating happily with each splurge. He imagined the glasses sliding off his nose with the persistent tremor. He played that game until he almost went under the wheels of an oncoming truck.

Found dead with my dick in a KFC bucket, he said aloud to himself, I might make the papers.

Two Häagen-Dazs tubs (Strawberry Cheesecake, Bailey's Irish Cream) and a plastic bag that he only noticed the air holes in once *it was too late to stop. He considered the warning to keep plastic bags away from children printed on the side as his shoe filled up and his sock got warmer.*

At the Motel 6, he pushed his hair back from his eyes and lay on his bed. He took the bible from the bedside cabinet and tore its pages out until he tired of the mess. He sat at the edge of the bed and pulled his boots off with a grunt, reaching for the TV remote. One of the cable channels was playing some adventure movie which he thought he recognised, he watched it listlessly, propped up on his pillows, eating the packet of M&Ms that sat propped up on his chest. Intermittently they rolled away and disappeared beneath his torso. He was surprised to see the rescue scene on his TV dissolve into a soft-core coupling, the diminutive blonde girl sitting atop her rescuer grinding him gratefully into the dirt, his hat snatched from his head to frame her pretty face.

He sat up and reached for the cable menu on top of the TV.

Dick Champ is the Sexy Explorer in Poon Raider, he read aloud bemusedly, full hardcore version available after 9pm.

He glanced at the screen to admire the careful editing that let the viewer think he was experiencing something he was not. It wasn't even lunchtime so he settled back on the bed as Dick Champ cracked his whip and bucked insurmountable odds. He could hear the admiring gasps of the next girl he'd saved turning into something more as he succumbed to sleep.

Song 6: Porn

In his dream Death was at the door complaining about the flies buzzing around his face. He attempted to wave them away with a long skeletal hand, but they persisted, floating in and around his hooded skull, disappearing in and out of the black maw shrouding his features, darting around the dull red gleam of his eyes. I'm tired, said Death, tired of this, tired of carrying all this sadness around with me. Death pulled back his long grey and black coat to reveal a ribcage filled with rows of gleaming teeth, dried, curling ears like slender cuts of meat and fat wet tongues. Cut, said the Director with a sigh.

He'd been daydreaming again.

He looked down at the twinkling eyes and brilliant teeth of his co-star, Trina Topps. Her bulging, silicone breasts sat as two giant, austere orbs on his thigh, the pink skin pinched around their base like an old woman's mouth. I have to stop thinking like that, he thought, it doesn't help. She flashed him a smile and all he saw was the greying roots of her dull auburn hair, the spidery lines around each eye. His dick lay against his stomach, pallid and soft, gleaming dully with globs of Trina's spit. He sat up dazed, someone handed him a towel, Trina gave him a wink as she wrapped a robe around herself, her tits unmoving, slowly disappearing beneath the folds of white cotton. Her nipples looked like drink coasters and were about as sensitive, he thought. He surveyed the room around him (they were in someone's palatial bungalow, behind two gigantic dark wooden doors studded with iron knots, ugly, mostly white leather furniture, far too many plants and a pool at the back clogged with leaves from the boughs of the overhanging trees) and shook the thought away like a dog with wet ears. Bobby was staring at him. Bobby was the director. You okay? he asked. If I were okay we'd have finished the scene, he thought, but he answered instead with a shrug, tightening the towel around his waist. The room smelt of sweat, it felt clammy, he walked into the kitchen and placed both hands on the worktop, he wondered why they hadn't cleaned the water in the pool, it looked like it was filled with hair, the spindly leaves and pieces of bark set as dark, swirling spots on its surface.

He'd first made his name in the San Fernando Valley with a series known as The Cocksman Movies. Eight in all where he, as rutting, strutting Dick Champ (that was his billing, who came up with that he thought, smiling thinly in spite of himself) parlayed his way, usually with his dick in his hand or someone else's, through a series of big budget scenarios – big budget by the standards of the porn industry at least. He'd been the lusty

Indiana Jones, or his equivalent, in Poon Raider (hadn't a girl been bitten by a snake on set and sued the studio? It was all hazy; scenarios of convulsing flesh, tan lines and pumping fists merging in his mind), he'd dodged boulders, cracked his whip, fought and seduced Nazis and ended one scene with a girl wearing his fedora as she sat astride him, her hips making urgent, fervent circles as he lay there still inside her.

Indiana (or Dick Champ – The Sexy Explorer as the sleeve proudly proclaimed) was his favourite, he liked the outfit; he'd stolen the leather jacket after the shoot. The trousers were no good though, they were designed to come apart at the seams. He'd played Lord Invader in their Star Wars homage, that's what they called their thinly veiled, sodden remakes of contemporary classics; a homage. In the unimaginatively titled Sex Wars he'd spent half the film in PVC leggings that smelled second-hand and a doctored motorcycle helmet with a blackened visor that meant he was slick with sweat before every take. He'd grown to hate Lord Invader and his wheezing demeanour and consequently, the Star Wars franchise too. He only had to hear the familiar trumpeting theme before he flicked channels. They were the big moneyspinners though; they caught the editorial eye of Variety; to his equal delight and dismay the magazine ran a photo of him; unfortunately, it was a cropped picture of him delivering one of many money shots, his face contorted into a paroxysm of sexual delight. It looked like he'd been kicked in the stomach. For a while there were rumours of the big studios suing them, but it came to nothing. Consequently, both titles garnered cult status, showing as a double bill late on Friday nights in some mainstream cinemas. He'd been invited on to the Howard Stern Show, Howard told him he knew something about being sued himself while his production team made honking sounds and played hysterical canned laughter as he sat there utterly bemused.

You're a big guy, right? asked Howard. I'm tiny, I mean, I'm like a mouse, could I get a gig in porn? I mean, he leered; some of those chicks are hot.

He'd met a publisher at a party who broached the idea of him writing his autobiography. Maybe later, he countered, when I'm done with this life or it's done with me. They both laughed, clinking glasses as the party moved around them in the beaming faces of their fellow guests, girls stealing second glances at him, not sure where they knew him from, but that they did somehow. That was strong currency in this town.

He could remember the first time it happened or didn't happen. He'd worked with Kristal and Bunnie before. Two diminutive blondes who sometimes doubled up to play the part of sisters. They weren't of course, but the idea made them easier to sell. As the Crystal Sisters they were always the hot ticket for autographs at sex expos for long lines of bubble-shaped men in polo shirts and loafers. He didn't understand where the name came from and when he asked Bunnie she told him that it rhymed, stupid. She was giggling as she said it, she was always giggling, her perpetually gleaming mouth daubed in bright lip gloss. Kristal had appeared in Poon Hunter, he'd rescued and then seduced her, or had she rescued him and then he'd seduced her as a thank you, he couldn't recall. Very James Bond if that had been the case, he thought. The girls even had their own DVD hit with Sisters Under the Skin; he had no idea what the title meant either, but then he imag-ined it didn't worry them or their audience. It didn't matter, he liked them solo, but he liked them working together best. We're going to tag team you, they'd say before the director called out action. Kissing him sweetly on the cheek as if he were dropping them home after a date.

He'd been flirting with the bank teller, glancing down and then up to hold her gaze as she sat behind the partition opposite him, when she sat up straight her eyes flickered above the glass pane. Let me just check your account. She wore a lingering smile as she said it, she sounded playful as if they were sharing a secret. He smiled broadly back, toying with the idea of asking her out. Conversely, even pornstars wanted to date, though dates could be difficult when the conversation came round to what he did for a living. Some women thrived on the fact; others were repulsed, their faces wrinkling in horror, hands tightening around their drinks. Occasionally, they simply chose not to believe him. Once, a girl dragged him to the nearest video store; their dinner sat on the table next to hastily scattered twenty-dollar bills, scouring the adult section until she came across one of his films. She stood there clutching the case, glancing from the sleeve to him and then back again in utter disbelief. So like, she asked, are you famous? You've answered that yourself, he said, suddenly emptied of excitement or anticipation.

So, anyway, he started to say, nervously fingering the chain on the pen attached to the desk when he felt a shot of pain piercing his back, flaring up between his shoulder blades. Light spilled into his eyes and exited through his temples as the bridge of his nose crashed into the lip of the teller's desk. He felt blood filling his mouth like rusty spit and caught the panic in the girl's eyes as he started to slide toward the polished wooden floor.

Down, shouted the voice, everyone down, he smiled sluggishly, wanting to tell this stranger that he was down already, anyone could see that. The stranger stood over him, he was waving a handgun about and he had a red ski mask on that made him look like a paunchy Spiderman, his chins spilling out from under the cotton. We never did a porn superhero, he thought as he lay there feeling supine and warm, he liked the idea of wearing a cape. He had once played a criminal, a kidnapper whose victim had fallen for her captor. Just like in that Almodóvar film, he said to the director who regarded him so blankly that he wasn't sure he'd heard him and then decided on reflection that he almost certainly had.

The stranger was saying something to the girl, he was yelling, waving the gun around, someone's beeper was going off. The stranger looked at him, it was his beeper. He waved weakly, tried to form an apology for the interruption and then for a moment there was stillness between them, the stranger regarding him almost quizzically, his head cocked like a parakeet's. Then he calmly looked away, levelled his gun at the girl and fired, the world fragmenting suddenly in a smoky red cloud. He heard screaming, the sound of people running, more gunshots, he felt warm blood on his face; he heard another beep, he had a message.

He felt the familiar warmth of Kristal's lingering kiss, he felt the gooey imprint of gloss on his cheek, she whispered good luck before tracing a perfectly manicured, perfectly fake nail across his torso and then the director called out places, and then action. He saw their darting tongues at his dick like lizards tasting the condensation in the air; he felt the pulse emanating from his thighs, the room slowing down in time with its thick beat. A bluebottle making lazy zigzagging shapes in his peripheral vision. Then another silently hovering into view above Bunnie, moving in time with her bobbing head, shifting in space to stay an inch or so above her halo of peroxide hair. He leant forward to wave it away and she shot him a suspicious glance as his hand swept past her head. He tried sitting up, but Kristal pushed her hand flatly against his chest and laid her body against his, easing him back on to the bed. Bunnie, resolute, ran her tongue against him and squeezed his balls a little harder than she might have needed to. She feels slighted, he thought, she thinks I was trying to make her stop. There was no sensation, he was removed and remote, he studied the brass curves of the ornate lamp hanging overhead, the portrait of a woman he didn't know on the wall. She was smiling keenly, a laugh at her lips as if the painting had been copied from a photograph; the sea was behind her, sand at her feet. He thought about her at the beach, waving into the lens, smiling broadly before she turned and threw herself into the water and towards the horizon, strong, assured strokes breaking the waves. He wondered about the people who hired out their homes to the adult industry, he wondered about the rates, who cleaned up after them, did they come home to the pungent scent of sex and sodomy? The lamp was crawling with flies, the painting obscured, an occasional oil rendered eye appearing through the throng. He felt that the gaze was an admonishing one.

★   ★   ★

You didn't even know the girl at the bank, his agent said to him. People aren't going to hire a guy that, you know. He mimicked a firing pistol with his thumb and index finger. The problem is up here, said his doctor, tapping his forehead with a pencil. He sat there on the examination table, naked apart from his socks and a disposable tunic that wouldn't quite meet at the back. He swung his feet like a child; the leather top of the table was sticking to his bare legs. It's trauma, said the doctor, you suffered a terrible trauma, but there was nothing you could have done. He would have killed that girl whether you were there or not. Your beeper going off only delayed the inevitable. You're not to blame. He looked at his doctor and found he was slowly nodding.

The room had exploded after that first series of shots. The back of the stranger's too tight leather jacket punctured by bullets; his torso convulsing with the violent rhetoric of the barking guns. He held on to the counter as his body shook, that's where I hit my face he thought, running his tongue along the inside of his lip, it tasted salty, a tooth felt chipped. The dead weight of the stranger brought him slowly down. He bent at the middle like a folding chair and settled across him, his mask had ridden up a little and he could see that he had a moustache. He reached out and cradled his head, laying his hand along the cheek. Get back, someone said and then more urgently, get back, get back.

He sat home most nights, watching old friends and associates work their sticky magic on his TV set. There was Bunnie at her cheery best; legs taut, mouth in an everlasting O. His hand rummaged in his boxer shorts anticipating the twinge he had always felt in the company of his fellow actors. Sometimes he'd wake up, the cheerful Californian sun blazing across the valley, his bedroom lit in a soft orange light, his dick pushing against the cotton sheets, upright. But a piss would deflate it; a tentative caress would be enough to make it loll sadly to one side.

He drove around at nights, visiting the stores that stocked his films. He locked himself into a viewing booth once, the smell of cleaning fluid pinching at his nose, causing his eyes to water, and fed money into the slot and watched Dick Champ battle evil and rob graves as The Sexy Explorer. He was surprised and impressed by the production values, but not as much as he was by his insatiable desire, his eagerness to consume, his girth, the weight, the heart of him driven on, plunging in again and again.

He sat in the parking lot of the bank and watched the tellers leave for the night. He listened to the clicking of their heels, watched the muted colours of their pencil skirts diminishing with distance into the muggy twilight, their hair pinned up on their heads, loose strands brushing their shoulders. He thought about marrying one of them, but he'd tried dating again; receptionists, waitresses, lawyers, the outcome was always the same. Those who weren't repulsed by his past (conversely, there were some dates far too eager to relive it, some wanted to watch his films with him and would ask him to pass comment on the parade of blow jobs and girls; he was a DVD extra before such things existed) eventually couldn't reconcile themselves with it. When, ultimately, they got to the point of intimacy he couldn't rouse himself – the last time he'd had penetrative sex was with a Texan girl who called herself Red on the set of a film called One Trick Pony – they blamed themselves for not being cast in the porn starlet mould. But ordinary is what I want he'd said once in the gloom between night and the oncoming morning, reaching out and then he caught the girl's crumpled, trembling features in the dusky light and her wretchedness made him want to cry out. He held her until the day rose in a warm wave along his back and across his shoulders.

He felt his life becoming smaller and smaller, at least the bluebottles have stopped coming, he said out loud and quite alone. In his hands he cradled an old, neo-antique shotgun he'd bought three days before. Guns made him nervous, even replicas that he'd handled on set. He found himself admiring its long, steely barrels, the raised nub that constituted the sight. He'd hold it up, train it along the valley below, trace the line of a car in the distance and imagine himself picking off pedestrians and drivers alike, watching cars careening out of control, the shattering glass and wrench of steel silent and displaced this far away as if none of it were his fault, that his actions had no consequence. Not that this would have the range, he said, admiring the stock and shape of the gun. He broke it open, pushed two cartridges into the twin burnished tubes, closed it again and enjoyed the mechanism, the deft click. Then he put the end in his mouth, placing the butt on the floor. I was seventeen when I first came out here, he thought, I'll be thirty-three when I leave. He admired the barrels again; they were untiring, hard against his lips. There would be a spark, an ignition and then life and death in one fiery bloom. He tensed his back and closed his eyes and leant forward to depress the trigger to lead him from this world into the next. His hand scrabbled for the key to the exit and there was a moment in which blue-bottles swirled and batted against the window and Death sat hunched across from him, his baleful gaze unmoving, the red of his eyes picked out in the black. Then the moment passed, the air was clear and he sat back, tears on his cheek, he looked along the length of the gun before realising with a sound that was caught somewhere between sobbing and laughter that he couldn't reach the trigger.

Down in the valley a car skidded out of control, people panicked and ran; someone was shooting at the highway.

Chorus

The film was finished and Dick Champ spent when the driver finally woke to find night filling the small oblong window of his room. He rolled over and opened the drawer beside his bed, switching the lamp on into dull life as he did so. He found the phonebook and flicked through the thick swathe of cardboard-coloured pages. His fingers idly traced the numbers.

The last time he'd made an anonymous call, he'd convinced the woman at the other end of the phone that her husband had been downloading child pornography on to his computer.

No, she gasped and he'd heard her grip loosen on the receiver.

But he's at work all day, she stammered.

They let him go, he replied, weeks ago. After they'd found the pictures on his hard drive. He paused significantly. He didn't tell you? he asked.

But we have two girls, she said, her voice breaking, punctuated by tears.

I know, he said, that's why I'm calling you. We've got him here, he said, then he paused and then he rang off, falling back on to the motel bed and laughed.

He had a theory, he had a number of theories, he'd tried a few out on his shrink before he'd finally left town, but the shrink would interrupt him (he called it interjecting) to make it clear that he didn't like the direction the conversation was taking. It wasn't, he'd suggest, healthy. His theories, sometimes formulated in the car on the way to his appointments, were designed with his shrink in mind. He'd long got bored of the sessions, of being asked to reveal pivotal points about his childhood (the shrink would sit forward in his seat when he spoke about being a kid, once he laid a distracted hand on his shoulder), but he enjoyed visiting his therapist for other reasons. He'd begun to treat it as a series of mental exercises. Now those weekly visits were one of the few things he missed about his old life in New Jersey.

He was testing a theory again, one he really believed in. His therapist was making a steeple with his fingers. It was, he thought, the kind of thing the therapist might have seen in a film once and considered iconic, the therapist wasn't averse to affectation. He wore glasses he didn't need and always wore his tie loose, his top button casually opened at his throat. His therapist, he had concluded, was an insecure sap; he couldn't fuck with him enough, but this theory he was expounding was a theory he believed.

Some people, he said, go through life like they're driving bumper cars. You know what a bumper car is, he asked his therapist. His therapist nodded, he was using two fingers to work the knot loose on his tie.

Like at a carnival! the therapist said.

Right, he said, like at a carnival. Some people treat their lives like they're driving new cars, others like they're at the wheel of a hire car, for some it's the bumper car, do you follow me? he asked, though he knew his therapist didn't.

How often do people get a new car in their lifetime? he asked the therapist, I mean regular guys, not people like you and me. He smiled as he said it.

They pet that car, nurture it, clean it at weekends, cover the seats in plastic. Ever put plastic on your car seat? He didn't wait for him to answer. Then they drive the car, he searched for a word, tentatively, give it a name, pat the dashboard, wish it good morning and good night, convince themselves that if they love it enough then other drivers will love and respect it too when it's out there on the road or parked alone in a poorly lit street. As if loving something hard enough could save it from harm.

The therapist nodded, he was cleaning his glasses.

Why do you have those he asked, indicating the glasses.

I need them, said the therapist and held them up to the light before putting them back on.

Pure fucking theatre, he thought, giving his therapist a level gaze, but he said nothing.

The cars, your theory, said the therapist. It was quiet in the office, they were too high up to even hear the constant thrum of traffic below.

What do you drive? he asked.

I'm not sure that's important, said the therapist. It hasn't got a name though. He smiled thinly.

I bet it's a BMW, he said to the therapist, I bet you tell people you drive a beamer and I bet it has got a fucking name. There was a pause, his therapist wrote something in his notebook.

Why don't you drive yourself into the city? the therapist asked.

That's my driver's job, he said sullenly. *He needs the work. Besides, I'm no good in the city. I react badly to other drivers. I like space when I'm behind the wheel, not the constant shuffling of cars idling from red light to red light, it makes me tense.*

The therapist examined the back of his head intently as if he'd never seen him or it before.

And how does that manifest itself? the therapist asked.

Do you want to hear my theory or not? he replied tersely. *It's a good one.*

He glanced back at him, their eyes met. The therapist nodded.

So, he continued, *some people live their lives like it's a new car they're driving, they're wary of every step, assume that the next corner will lead to an accident, they tread,* and he paused significantly, *carefully. Then the second group, the next group,* he continued, *life to them is like a hire car, a nick here, a bump there, but not too much, no one wants to lose their deposit, you know.*

He looked at his therapist. *You ever hire a car and get out of town?* he asked him.

Of course, said the therapist, *a few times.*

Ever take a hire car, hit someone when you're drunk, maybe kill them and to cover your tracks, set fire to it and run it off a cliff then report it stolen? he asked him.

No, said the therapist.

Me neither, he said.

But for some people, he continued, *the hire car, that's living. Taking a corner too fast, fucking in the back, not caring where you come on the upholstery, smoking at the wheel and dumping the ash down behind the seat. It's not like you have to valet the thing. It's the flashes of light that shine down into the darkness of your life, those moments of freedom. People relish that chance of freedom but only once they've realised they relinquished it somewhere. Do you think you're free? he asked.*

I'm not sure that's important, said the therapist. Do you?

My father's death made me free, financially at least. Do you want to hear about people who drive bumper cars? They're my favourite.

The therapist's nod was almost imperceptible this time.

They go through life with the most choices, he said. Because they choose whether to hit the other cars or not, hell, they don't even know when they're going to get hit. They don't live their lives by any recognisable design, a template, a blueprint, you know. They react to things around them, it's instinctive, and do you know what the greatest thing about people in bumper cars is? he asked.

The therapist shrugged, conceding he did not.

Anyone can drive a bumper car, he said with relish, all it takes is a run of bad luck or the death of a child, a marriage that's turned ugly, money problems. Once people tip that first domino and assume the worst is going to happen then it's easy for them to stop caring about the other guy on the road. A fender bender here becomes a clipped wing mirror there, a drunken fatality, a three-car pile-up. It all starts with one step, one drink too many on the drive home, like any great journey. He grinned recklessly. Come on, he said, you don't need to wear those fake fucking glasses and tighten up that tie.

He sat up on the bed and thought about the calls he'd already made: the one about the husband getting himself off on child pornography; a wife dead in a car crash out on the interstate; he'd tell people he knew they were alone and he was watching the house; he'd leave messages on answer-phones to tell people that their children had been dredged up dead and bloated in the nearest river; that an errant husband had been caught with his dick in a prostitute. It was, he truly believed, his way of setting people free, plus, he reasoned, he really liked fucking with people.

He settled on a number and made himself comfortable, he took a long pull on his drink and dialled the number, it rang briefly and was then snatched from its receiver. The voice at the other end sounded haunted and reckless. He thought of a fairground again, the brightly coloured bumper cars juddering on impact, the rain of sparks bursting into life against the wire mesh overhead. He remembered once standing on the raised lip of the ride as the cars trundled past and he stepped off and into their path.

The voice at the end of the line spoke first.

Where is she? he demanded to know, where's my wife? Delighted, he decided to play along. He took another quick hit on his bottle and decided to play the petulant child.

That's what I want to know; he could feel his voice tightening, going up a note, where is she? He felt hysterical himself, exhilarated, the skin on his arms prickled into life.

I'm her husband, raged the voice at the end of the phone, her husband. He sounded small and wounded.

He laughed absurdly knowing he'd found a strange confidant, someone to share his pain with. This was someone who was already out of control, shunting his way through life, scattering people, ignoring their screams. In another life, he thought, he would have liked him; they could have stared down the terror together, exacted revenge on unfaithful wives and girlfriends.

Let me tell you about your wife, he said. He looked down at the phonebook to check he'd got the right name. Raven, listen to me, that bitch isn't just fucking me, hell, she's running around on the guys that she's using to run around on you. She's fucking insatiable. She told me you were never enough for her. I guess I'm not either.

There was nothing but a subdued gurgling coming from the end of the phone, the sound of a grown man trying to conceal his tears. He thought about pressing on, but the fun had gone out of it, he needed the call and response of it, he needed the game, not mute compliance, the soft, bubbling sound of sadness. He placed the phone back in its cradle and let the world he'd destroyed go spinning off its axis quietly down the fibre-optic line, all that anger and hate minuscule and tiny and shrinking with every quiet second.

He'd set Raven free, he reasoned. But he felt itchy and desperate to be on the road again. He stalked around the ever-darkening room and began throwing clothes into his bag. The receptionist looked surprised to see him checking out in the middle of the night, but said nothing as the driver paid his bill in crumpled dollars and pushed out of the door without looking back. He was in a hurry, he muttered as he left, he had to get back on the road.

Song 7: House

Oh, you'll like this one, said the realtor, her hand flitting between her thigh and the gear stick.

She smiled as she said it, her mouth was a gleaming welcome sign, a strong, unflinching beam. He hated her within minutes of their meeting, especially as he realised he couldn't maintain his loathing when confronted with her perfect face. Her every utterance pricked at his skin, but her eyes confounded him and brought out a drooling adolescent compliant and eager to please. Every property so far had the greatest view, the greatest rooms; he prepared himself to be dazzled as he passed through yet another door that framed only disappointment. He nodded happily back at her as they came across yet another dimly lit box room after she'd promised him what sounded like high-vaulted atriums stuffed with pillows.

The streets went by in avenues and crossroads, rusting rails and white wooden fences, overgrown gardens, cars backed up in twos in their driveways. She was talking again; he wished she'd shut up and turn the radio on.

Mr Raven next, she said as they got out of the car and took the steps up to the porch.

Like the bird, she grinned as she pushed at the doorbell.

Idiot, he thought, but he was wearing an immoveable grin as he watched her take the steps as quickly as her closely fitted skirt would allow. She was beautiful in a hermetically sealed sort of way. He wanted to prise her casing apart and fall on the soft flesh beneath.

She pressed the bell again, there was no response and for a moment he saw the slightest downturn in her mouth.

Odd, she said in a voice without colour, a voice that wasn't used to disappointment, that was used to getting its own way. She would, he thought, use that voice if she woke up one morning and found blood and bones in her hair. She took out her cell phone and stabbed at the buttons. He was impressed by her dexterity. Inside the property a phone rang, he imagined himself inside the walls regarding the ringing phone. There was a pause and then the sound of something hitting the wall that caused them to take a step backwards.

She looked at him. She wasn't smiling. The phone stopped ringing, which caused her to stare quizzically at her cell phone as if she'd caused it to cease.

Hello, someone said, he could hear the tiny voice buzzing from her handset. It was hard to imagine the owner of that voice standing beyond this very door; he sounded a hundred miles away.

Mr Raven, she said. She was sparkling again, all neon and cleavage, it's Julie Ledger, the realtor? we have a viewing.

As if to emphasise the point, she leant in on the doorbell again, the sound of it came back minuscule and remote through her cell. They heard the sound of the phone going down both inside the house and out.

Mr Raven's voice came through the wood and small glass panel of the door. Julie Ledger was craning forward to see inside, she quickly looked down at her shoes as his face appeared in the square window set head height in the door.

I can't just now, said Mr Raven, the place is in a real mess. His head turned as if he were surveying a room in sudden violent disarray and seeing it all for the first time.

We don't mind a little mess, said Julie Ledger. He imagined tiny bells ringing when she spoke.

Mr Raven . . . She rang the buzzer again for good measure even though they were now almost eye-to-eye through the glass. He had to give it to her; her smile was still so fixed that she looked like a skull.

Stillness, a car went by, a dog barked, suburbia drifted along in these innocuous streets, he looked around, he liked it, it reminded him of being twelve years old. He could pitch a baseball on these neat, oblong lawns, drink a beer. He was never happier than when he felt like he was living the life of an actor in a commercial. He liked their summation, their precise message, that the story they had to tell was related in thirty or forty seconds and then gone. He imagined their happiness behind his TV screen; they lived out here somewhere beneath these blue skies, their lives lit up with the wonder of promise.

The door opened, Mr Raven appeared as if in section, a sliver of his sweating face visible through the opening.

You can't come in, he said. He sounded unsure himself. Miss Ledger, sensing his vulnerability, pushed at the door, but it stuck fast and she bounced back a little harder than she might have liked. She studiously ignored it, like someone losing their footing on ice in front of a restaurant window full of diners would.

Mr Raven, she insisted, her voice colder, then in a tone that was both patronising and pleading.

My client, she indicated him standing there. Did he imagine that she bowed her head when she did this? She was suddenly cowed. How many parts could she play? he wondered. His eyes drifted down to her tough-looking calves. Works out, he thought. He admired her loosely pinned hair, her painted nails, no wedding ring, he glanced at his bare fingers, he hadn't worn his ring since the divorce. Sometimes during his frequent indiscretions: that was how he referred to the infidelities that broke his marriage apart, indiscretions, it was a word that took the guilt and madness out of his actions, he'd slide the ring off and drop it into his pocket. If he forgot he was wearing it and it came up in conversation then he'd tell the woman it was a family heirloom, that he wore it to remember his grandfather by and then he'd slide into the seat next to them.

There was a moan and then a syrupy-sounding cough as if someone's mouth was filled with thick liquid. Mr Raven suddenly disappeared from view and they both leant forward to make out the dark shapes moving around behind the door. Mr Raven's face came hurriedly back into view.

I've got someone sick in here, he said. He looked resigned and frightened as if he'd slipped out over some unimaginable edge and it was too late to gain a foot or handhold and drag himself back to safety.

Mr Raven, Julie Ledger said again, but he could tell her heart wasn't in it. She looked tired suddenly; her shoulders sloped so that the front of her buttoned jacket pointed outwards.

We'll have to make another appointment, said Mr Raven, quietly composing himself. He ran his hand over his face to wipe the sweat away; it looked like it was smeared in tar, his fingernails black. He closed the door with a resounding thud and they both stood there in the silence, dust from the porch clouding their ankles and feet. He was about to suggest that they creep around to the back of the house and peer in the windows to still the uneasy feeling in his stomach when she spoke.

I'm so sorry about that. I remember when me and my roomy came down with flu, we couldn't bear the thought of visitors; we had tissues and empty orange juice cartons everywhere. She smiled, she trilled, she made some sort of throwaway gesture with her hands, he wanted to choke her until she fell to her knees and pleaded with him to stop.

Don't you think something's going on, he said, something bad?

Oh please, she said, her indestructible smile had returned. People get ill all the time. And with that she strode off the patio and towards her car. She turned to him and held the beeping car door open.

Momentarily he heard the buzzing of the electricity wires overhead and a window shutting somewhere. Everything was in vivid relief, the blades of grass in the back yard shimmered with green light and sang, there was a haze to them that hurt his eyes, it felt as though there was someone standing close to him and the light was drawn up and out of the house and the silence and sky were suddenly flat and lifeless. The unearthly buzz sparked off and fell around him like sudden rain. Julie Ledger leant on the car horn.

Come on, silly, she said, we've still got one more house to see, and her smile was an opening, her body an invitation, he felt a surge of longing as she dropped her head slightly and held out a hand to him.

Business first, she said, then pleasure.

The next time he passed the house it was done up like a hastily wrapped gift in a crisscross of black and yellow police tape. He felt his stomach lurch as he drove by, slowing down to take in the garish panorama. The house was ugly, more so than he remembered, and he found his eyes drawn to the overhead wires. He remembered the figure out in the garden and the shadow that it cast along the yard and up and over the house and then the stillness that consumed him. He pulled over and went and stood in front of the house, he touched the tape and felt himself tip slightly, the air sucked from his lungs, spots of light darting in front of his eyes. The policeman came from around the back of the house, took the stairs slowly and stood looking at him, one hand on his hip, near his holster. He flicked the button that opened it up to reveal the dark brown of the revolver handle beneath.

Sir, said the policeman evenly, this is a crime scene. He indicated the tape ringing the perimeter fence and house like weeds strangling a flower. Could you please step back. The policeman stared gravely down at his hands which he realised were clutching the tape as if it might hold up him up if he started to fall. He slowly let go and stood there gulping for air.

What happened? he said. The policeman was detached and remote, he was still like a cat, he said nothing.

I was here, he said softly, and the colour came flooding back into the policeman's eyes as if he were focusing for the first time.

Sir, the policeman said, lifting the tape and stepping under it, did you say you were here? The policeman gently placed his gloved hand on his wrist and let it stay there.

I'm not going to run away, he said, but he didn't know if that were true. I was here looking at the house a few days ago and Mr Raven . . .

You knew Mr Raven, said the policeman; he stepped closer and tightened his hand a little around his wrist.

He came to the door, he said. He was sweating, there was tar on his hands. There was someone moving around inside. We heard them coughing and there was someone standing out in the yard. He tried to point to the back of the house to indicate where he meant, where he'd dreamt of playing ball, but the policeman held his arm tightly.

We? the policeman said.

The realtor, he said. She wanted me to rent the place, my wife had thrown me out, I needed somewhere to live.

He was crying suddenly, leaning against the policeman for support, his body convulsing and shaking until he felt empty. The policeman gently pushed him back onto his feet and then led him to the police car that was parked two spaces from his.

★   ★   ★

127

He saw Julie Ledger through the glass and in spite of himself felt his heart lurch. The detective opposite him followed his gaze.

Cute, the detective said. Is that why you didn't report what happened at the house, too busy sniffing around after her?

No, he said, but he meant yes. We were looking at houses, he said.

Tell me again, said the detective, how you heard something, someone maybe, hit the wall of the house, saw blood on Mr Raven's hands . . .

I thought it was tar, he said.

You thought it was tar, said the detective. What did you think you heard hitting the wall, the bucket the tar came in?

I didn't know what it was, he said.

You said you wanted to go to the back of the house to check what was going on. Why didn't you? said the detective.

We had another house to see, he said, but he had no resolution left, he felt shallow and ashamed. He'd felt the life going out of that house and into the sky and had done nothing about it. Instead he'd followed Julie Ledger to her car, driven to the next apartment which he neither liked nor wanted but had signed off on regardless as Miss Ledger had intimated (he imagined, had he imagined it?) that doing so might mean that their mutual business was out of the way and any more time they spent together would be purely for pleasure.

She'd driven him to her office, his eyes roaming her body with every carefree mile, where he'd signed the six-month lease and then she'd walked him to where his car was parked at the rear of her building. The wind had picked up and caused her shirt to pull tightly against her, he felt thrilled standing there as if he could lean in and kiss her and she'd return it, her warm mouth on his. Instead, she brusquely shook his hand, thanked him for his business and hoped that he'd be happy in his new home. It was then he saw the glinting engagement ring come to life on her finger.

Your ring, he said stupidly as his face got hot.

I never wear it when I'm working, Miss Ledger said brightly. Imagine if I lost it looking round a property, I'd never forgive myself. She smiled and it was a smile that said our business is finished here, go away, you're staring and it's creeping me out.

You thought you saw someone in the garden, said the detective.

I don't know, he said, it was more of a feeling. He felt useless thinking it, let alone saying it.

So you didn't see anyone in the garden, said the detective, but you said you thought you did?

A man came into the room and handed the detective a folder. She's got nothing, he said, indicating Julie Ledger beyond the glass and then looked at him for a moment.

Not according to our friend here, said the detective and waved the folder in his direction. Both men smiled and the man who'd brought the folder in left, he held the door open briefly and he could hear an electronic typewriter clatter and ping and someone ask for coffee, black, and then the door closed and it was quiet again.

You're dead from the eyes up, were the last words she said, that's when Mr Raven hit her. She bounced off the wall and crashed into the couch, but then came up fast attacking his face with both hands. They struggled for a moment and he could feel the sweat forming on his neck. He pulled his hand back and hit her in the side of the head and she staggered, gave him a murderous look and sank to the floor, blood gathering around her nose and lips.

In the last year of their marriage she'd taken lovers, as had he, as their marriage had waned and their sex life had shrunk. When they'd first bought the house they couldn't decide what colour to paint the bedroom so they'd daubed different colours on the wall, it was, they'd admit, a horrible mess, but they couldn't bear to paint over it. So for months they lay beneath a blur of colours and a jumble of half-hidden words, it was like sleeping as the walls exploded silently around them. Together they'd been as brilliant as those colours, now they were bleached like bones. They'd get drunk and talk about it some nights, wonder at the vagaries of love that had drawn them together and was now pushing them apart. They agreed to rent out their home and spend some time apart, hoping that in the spaces they left that love would flood in and buoy them both up again, the current causing their respective crafts to tip towards the other.

Then one night the phone rang and it was a man's voice. He was drunk and demanded to know where she was.

I'm her husband, he raged, her husband, but the man had laughed at him and told him what she had said about him behind his back when she was with him, when she was with all the other men. His own affairs simply wearied him, he took no pleasure in it, sex was revenge, but he wasn't sure against whom. Their drunken evenings became binges, their conversations screaming fights until one night she didn't come home. It was midday when she came through the door and the argument started almost instantly. By the time they'd finished fighting she was splayed unconscious on the floor, her leg gathered up underneath her as if she'd been pushed from the balcony of a tall building. Her face was covered in blood, the red seeping into her mouth. His hands were tacky with sweat, make-up and skin. Then the doorbell rang and then his phone and then he was standing at his door trying to persuade two strangers to leave. His head was pounding, the walls pulsed and boomed, he could barely hear what the girl outside the door was saying, the wires overhead sang and then the silence snapped as his wife came spluttering back into life. He rushed to her side and forced his fingers into her mouth and clutched her throat with his free hand until she sank back into blackness then realising the door was still open he flung himself into the space, his heart threatening to burst from his chest. There was blood on his fingers. He could feel it.

Once they'd finally gone, he sat there in the darkness of the lounge, feeling figures moving about outside, saw the shadows pressed against the windows. He went to the bedroom and opened the bedside cabinet and took out the revolver they kept there in case of intruders, placed it in his mouth and pulled the trigger. He saw the light leave his body as his head snapped back and he dropped into the corner and out of sight.

He killed her and then he killed himself, while you were outside, said the detective.

I didn't hear a gun go off, he said.

The detective looked squarely at him and tapped the folder's spine on the desk.

Maybe you missed the suicide then, he said, we didn't find those bodies for days. The autopsy said she was still alive, for a few hours more at least, we might have been able to save her. Then he stood up and without looking back he opened the door and left.

That night, wretched and drunk, he called up his estranged wife, but she wouldn't take the call, he got her machine three times and then on the fourth someone picked up and then slammed down the receiver and the next two times he called it was busy. He gave up after that and went back to his seat in the bar. At one point he slid his ring off his finger (now he didn't need it he wore it almost constantly) and approached a group of women sat at a table, but he misjudged the space around them and dipped his head in to their circle too fast with a slurred, exultant, Ladies! One girl's wine sloshed into her lap with the impact and he skulked away as they regarded him in silence. Knowing he shouldn't but not caring, he picked up his car and started the drive home to the new apartment that he hated. He felt queasy and parched. He wound down his window and navigated the darkened streets with a determination that saw him sat low in his seat, hands clenching the steering wheel. His mouth was so firmly set that his jaw hurt.

The black and yellow house came at him out of the darkness.

Police line, do not cross, he said quietly to himself as he stepped over the tape and up the steps towards the door. He stood there a moment, swaying slightly and looked in through the glass pane where Mr Raven had once looked back when he wasn't choking and beating his wife to death. He felt sadness and shame engulf him, felt the weight of his misguided lust settle firmly on his shoulders and he began to sag, he felt his

spine buckle and his knees begin to give. The police tape crossed
the door in an X as if the occupants were stricken by plague
and he pushed against it and felt it move slowly open. Inside
the room was dark and he moved clumsily to the sofa and sat
down heavily. He looked around in the gloom and wondered
where her body had lain as she choked slowly to death on her
own blood. How many feet away had he been staring lustily
at Julie Ledger as Mrs Raven had coughed and swallowed her
life away? He moved to the window that looked out on to
the garden at the back of the house and wondered what he
would have seen that day if he'd had the wherewithal to enter
the yard and peer into their lounge. Would Mr Raven have
been bent over his fading wife, his fingers reaching into her
mouth or would he have left the room by then in search of
his destiny at the end of a handgun? He moved to the bedroom,
eyes adjusting to the darkness, hands holding onto the walls. Their
bed was unmade and the sight of it made him unspeakably sad,
he crumpled against the dresser, catching her hairbrush and
knocking it to the floor. Suddenly he felt the warm flush of
tears. A voice came from the next room.

Come out of there with your hands up, this is a crime scene,
said the policeman from the living room. His gun was drawn
and when the weeping figure rushed at him, a shadow among
all the other shadows suddenly shouting, I was here, I was here,
I was here, he panicked and fearing for his own life he shot
into those shadows and the shadow disappeared as quickly as
if daylight had suddenly filled the room. The policeman holstered
his gun and stood over him feeling for a pulse where there
was none. His head was turned to one side and there were still
tears on his cheek. The policeman called it in and shaken sat

back on the sofa and tried to slow his breathing and the incessant thumping in his chest while he waited for the ambulance and help to arrive.

Out in the yard, Death yawned solemnly, pulled back the heavy folds of his long coat and scratched absently at a gleaming rib; soon, he thought, it'll be time to go.

Chorus

The emergency phones dotting the road towards Las Vegas were powered by compact, spidery-looking solar panels attached like black antennae to their frames, peering upward and reaching out to the sky above them.

Good luck if you break down out here, said the driver to himself. It's like the surface of fucking Mars.

He retuned his radio again and again only to come back to a quasi country music show with religious overtones and redemption in every zealous link that the DJ made. He'd start out sounding like he was pitching a sale and then you'd realise that he was selling only one thing: salvation. It made the driver feel creepy, as if he had an unwanted guest in the car; a hitchhiker suddenly determined to save his soul even if that meant taking it. He pushed the image from his mind and let the brimstone and fire wash over him. It was the only signal *he could find out there in the Nevada desert, though he couldn't imagine where they were broadcasting from or the power of their antennae, maybe from the sky itself. He turned the radio off and listened to his wheels turn.*

His darkened windows muted the daylight and he felt removed from his surroundings in the plush interior of his Lexus. The car, black inside and out, was something he'd bought not long after he'd come into his father's money. He wanted something that was somehow expressionless, but that also said stay away. His driver had laughed when he told him this, when did you start thinking that a $50,000 car was expressionless? he asked. It screams, Steal me, take me joyriding, leave me burning at the edge of a deserted road somewhere. Though no one ever had. He barely drove it into the city and at night he had his driver lock it securely away. Not that anyone ever intruded on his property, the house and its grounds still inspired intimidation and fear in people just like his father once had.

He'd had a blow-out on the outskirts of town, his back right tyre bursting into and out of life, sending his car spinning around in a half-circle to face the way he'd just come. The explosion it made caused him to duck involuntarily as if there were suddenly gunfire zipping over his head. He got out and stood at the side of the road. He was beyond the desert now, but still had some way to go. Sweat gathered at the small of his back as he stood there.

He was on his knees working the wheel off, the spare propped against his thigh, when he saw the shadow cast across the car. He instinctively tightened his grip on the wrench and got ready to rail around and strike out. His jaw was set so tightly that his teeth hurt.

Need a hand? said a voice.

He glanced around. The stranger looked both confident and cocky, hands set on his hips as if he were about to use his body to form giant letters of the alphabet. His sunglasses were impenetrable, his mouth tight. He seemed to regard the driver, sizing him up.

I'm good, said the driver. It's almost fixed.

He indicated the deflated tyre that was very far from almost fixed, no matter how you looked at it.

I've got a car, said the stranger, I could drive you into town or to the nearest garage. His car sat at the side of the road, one door open like a wing.

How didn't I hear him pull up? thought the driver.

The stranger stood there, unmoving, a slight breeze playing around the edges of his jacket. He was utterly silent then, cool and remote, but he looked like he wanted something, as if there was something on his mind.

I'm good, said the driver firmly. He glanced in at the shadowy interior of his car and wondered where his gun was. He had vague memories of throwing it from the car, then he imagined dropping it on the highway and watching it bounce away, but it all felt hazy and dreamlike and he wasn't even sure that it wasn't just stuffed under the seat or in the glove compartment. He patted his back pocket and was reassured to feel his knife. He chose to wave the wrench around a little in order to make his point.

They stood there silently for a moment like two gunslingers waiting for someone to make the first move. Then the stranger stepped quickly forward and the driver took an involuntary step backwards, the wrench rising in his fist again. The stranger smiled and laughed a little, then walked back to his car.

He pulled up next to the driver, the engine bubbled quietly and the stranger raised his sunglasses and stared with dead, featureless eyes a little longer than was comfortable.

Last chance, said the stranger. You could be in town in no time at all.
He waved his sunglasses at the faint promise of Las Vegas somewhere
over the next hill.

Cold beer, he said, air conditioning, dancing girls. He smiled widely
and the driver thought briefly that if he were close enough then this stranger
might lean forward and bite him on the face. The smile turned to a leer.
Whatever your pleasure may be, the stranger said.

The driver laid the wrench on his car roof with a clatter and regarded
the stranger across the rooftop.

I'm good, really, he said evenly and watched the stranger shrug and
pull onto the road and away, his car wavering and indistinct in the
waves of heat rising up from the highway.

He changed the wheel as quickly as he could, his thoughts never far
from the road he was on. Waiting for the sound of a car returning,
pulling up next to his. Death stealthy and sudden at the hands of the
stranger, strangling the life out of him, his legs dancing as he was pulled
sharply backward into oblivion. He got behind the wheel and pushed
the car on, offering up a silent prayer for the spare tyre to hold. He'd
bypass Vegas, he thought. Hadn't that been where the stranger was
heading back to? He passed the city in daylight, its silver and glass
beacons standing in the distance and thought about what sort of terrors
lay there. He wondered if that was how Oz looked and if Dorothy
must have thought the same thoughts herself as she approached the
turrets and towers in fear and wonder.

The circles of cross ramps carried him towards and then away
from the city. He thought he'd taken the wrong road at one point and
felt the panic rise inside him as he found himself being pulled towards the
Strip and into downtown, but the road curved and then straightened
out and the city was suddenly climbing skywards to one side of him,
reflecting his speed in its shimmering blue windows as he gathered

momentum and pulled away to the west. He cracked a window and felt the warm air filling the car. Even with his sunglasses on he found he was starting to squint.

How long do you think it'll take for us to get to the coast? his passenger asked. He knew the voice before he turned to look at the seat next to him. He pushed his sunglasses up onto his head and let the sun stream into his eyes, hoping that the white light would burn through the heart of the car and leave only their ashes on the seats, like the black blossoms left behind on the walls of Hiroshima.

Think you can make it without getting lost? his passenger said. He checked in his mirror and then forced himself to look to his right. His father was staring out of the window, one foot up on the dashboard; he was wearing an old pair of Aviator sunglasses that the driver remembered his father losing one summer in the sea while they were vacationing in Florida. His father removed them and turned to look at him.

I thought you lost those, said the driver.

Nah, said his father, twirling them around between his fingers. What made you think that?

Down in Florida, he started and then stopped. Was he talking to a ghost? Were the approaching cars passing him and wondering who he was speaking to?

They were where I always left them, said his father, and pushed them back up onto the bridge of his nose. Look at these crazy fuckers living out here in the desert, his father continued, indicating the suburban houses that had attached themselves in strips to the city.

I know we lived out of town, but we had a little space, you know, he said. Then he set both feet up on the dashboard and eased his seat back.

Who the fuck would choose to live in a desert, what are they, *fucking towel heads? All other people are crazy,* he sighed, looking across at his son, *never forget that.*

He stared hard ahead wondering how something so unreal could be so tightly bound up in his reality.

Do you remember when you rescued me? he asked his father, but his father remained mute, stony-faced. He'd put his glasses back on and now it looked as though he were hiding behind them.

Are you sleeping, Dad? he asked. But his father just shushed him and told him to keep his eye on the traffic that was slowing up ahead. He shifted down a gear and forced himself to focus, his eyes drifting occasionally to the right only to dart quickly back into place when he realised that his father was still sitting there and sometimes he was staring right back.

Song 8: Holiday

His holiday mementoes – one for every time he'd killed – filled the shelves of his bedroom. The snowglobes were collected in neat rows, the floor lamp in the corner positioned so that it backlit the glass and plastic domes, bringing the floating silver flakes to life when he shook them and quickly set them down to capture the effect. Like a showman spinning plates on poles he'd frantically run the length of the room, grabbing and shaking the globes as he went, then throwing himself down on the bed to watch the snow settle on the tiny vistas and landmarks magnified in their slowly glittering worlds.

The first time he killed a man he was surprised by how long it took. He stood over him, slick with sweat, panting, gripping the hammer tightly in one hand, a piece of piping in the other. He noticed that his fingers ached, his hand felt like a claw for hours afterwards. He'd rattled a tattoo of blows along his victim's skull and shoulders, but the man had remained firmly on his knees, his arms across his head to shield him from the blows. He'd got him down with the first swing, the hammer glancing off his temple, but he'd been resilient after that as if staying hunched on one knee would finally set him free. The first woman, slight, blonde, drunk and compliant, up to a point, had been much quicker. By the time her face had changed from heated excitement to furious panic and fear it was too late. He left her marvelling at the fact that strangulation did cause the eyes to bulge and the tongue to poke out and turn blue. Like a lizard, he'd thought, or an alien. Nothing was set in stone though. He stabbed one man under the heart and he'd sighed as something popped sagging against him like a drunk at a Christmas party, falling slowly to the floor. One woman – the clear plastic bag over her head sucking frantically, forming a clear shroud against her features – staggered and swung her fist even as her body bounced off the hotel door. He'd written the words *struggle* and *instinct to survive* in his journal that night, still feeling profoundly moved by her display of strength. He hadn't thought about letting her live though. That would have defeated the object of the holiday, he would have gone home disappointed, as if it had rained all week or if he'd twisted an ankle jumping into the sea.

He liked hunting in cities, Seattle, Chicago, New York. In places like those he could relax and enjoy the sites too, depending on when he struck. He'd once killed on the first night that he'd landed, an opportunistic murder on a Californian beach down from the hotel. It was late and she'd been walking along the shore, her jeans were rolled up and she was barefoot.

He'd fallen into step with her, she was drunk and had argued with her friends, she told him. She was clinging to his arm as they walked away from the harbour lights, leaning into him as he pointed out distant constellations, most of them imagined. He picked up pieces of wood and pebbles and flung them out over the dark waters until they dropped toward the horizon and out of sight. They were both listening for the splash when he scooped up the fist-sized rock at his feet and swung it upwards to strike her in the face. He caught her as her head snapped back and her nose broke. He let her drop into the sand and then sat across her chest and stove in her head with the rock, glancing over his shoulder as his arm crashed down with a sure rhythm. His heart was racing as he dragged her body into the surf and under a nearby pier. He pulled her body under the water and jammed it in against the wooden leg of the pier and weighed it down with rocks. He studied her face beneath the water as the tide washed the blood from her shattered features; she was, he thought, still very beautiful. He pulled off his shirt to hide the blood and wrapped it around his hand, he walked up the beach towards the hotel's welcoming glow, thinking that if he hurried he might catch last call at the bar after he'd towelled off. He was whistling something, but he couldn't be sure what. He bought the snowglobe at the hotel's gift shop on his last day there; a plastic shark, swimming above the name of the resort picked out in starfish in the sand. He gave it a shake, held it up against the sunlight and admired the colours swirling around as the driver loaded his luggage into the cab.

He was eleven years old, the sun hurting his eyes as he sat on the beach straining to make out the figures in the water off in the distance. His shoulders were peeling, his hair clammy with sweat and stuck fast to his forehead. The sky was more white than blue, a great canvas above the holidaymakers standing on the beach, united like a show's chorus line at the edge of the stage looking out over their audience. Everyone was standing and facing the same way, eyes trained on the small boat out in the ocean. He remembered the lifeguard shouting as he threw himself at the surf, a woman in a swimming cap decorated with rubber flowers screamed and pulled a child to her pale belly, the fat on her arms was slick and wet, the crystals of salt gleaming on her skin. The men were leaning over his mother, concern masking their features; they were pushing down on her chest, seawater and mucus trailing from her nose. One of the men pulled something out of her mouth and threw it away; he muttered something to himself as he did so. He leant over her and closed his mouth on hers to breathe life into her body. Nothing happened for a moment. He felt his shoulders itch and picked at the thin curls of peeling skin and then one of the men sat back on the sand and he started to cry. He'd never seen a grown man cry before.

He tried to take a holiday at least twice a year. One usually somewhere in the US and one abroad. His work, as a creative director for a large charity, was mundane and only called for creativity when it came to managing campaign budgets. He'd often thought about killing the people around him, usually on themed Fridays when they came loudly back from lunch at the bar in the basement of their building, but he reserved his bloody malice for strangers. He'd once met a stewardess on a flight to a resort in Cancun and had seduced her and cut her throat on her layover at a hotel near the airport. Her throat made a hissing sound at first (one he'd become used to over the years though at first it had unnerved him) and then there was the gurgling, bubbling wound mingling with the sound of the jets taking off and landing at what seemed like feet above the flat roof over their heads. She, like the girl on the beach, had freed him up for the rest of the holiday. He'd sunbathed and swam zealously, journeying to the buoys lolling in the deep water that led out to the endless ocean. He'd rest there, one hand set against the bobbing float as he fell and rose in the swell and wonder how far his mother had gone before she realised the trouble she was in. The moment when she suddenly knew that she had gone too far. If he raised himself up in the water he could just see the distant, retreating beach and the rectangles of glass and brick that made up the blocks of hotels set rigidly along the coastline. The stewardess had that look he imagined in his mother's eyes; first misunderstanding and then horror, the legs kicking out, thrashing against the inevitable. He saw his mother pushing towards the shore, legs pumping frantically and uselessly against the current, but moving only backwards towards the deep. He'd caught the stewardess as she lunged for the door, she cracked her head on the TV as she toppled over and then he was on her, his knife finding her throat, the familiar reservoir of air seeping free and then the small fountain of blood covering his hands as her limbs juddered ever more slowly to a stop behind him.

Some vacations were more stressful than others. He'd considered Las Vegas a soft target; putting it off as a destination until he was sure he wanted the easy option of aimless, bovine-like holidaymakers setting up home in their RVs at the wrong end of the Strip or the strung-out stag parties roaming aimlessly downtown, hopelessly out of control, twitching with cocaine and excitement. Who would notice his mania among all that brilliantly lit madness? But Las Vegas had made him uncomfortable from the start, even behind the tinted windows of the town car taking him from the airport to his hotel he felt the searing heat coming off the desert, saw it raking at the sky. He felt breathless even with the air-conditioning, his sunglasses seemed opaque in the glare, even among the deep leather upholstery he felt unprotected. At the hotel he rushed straight to his room set high in one of its towers. He could see the city below him and then the mountains with their serrated edges blurred and softened by the heat.

He rented out a hire car and cruised the suburbs that buffered Las Vegas, always surprised by how close and how quickly the desert came rushing up to the city as if it was trying to reclaim the land the place was built on. He imagined a world where vegetation and dirt had enveloped the cities; tall buildings as a mass of creeping vines, the streets mud tracks, like a frontier town. He'd stopped to help or attack a man changing the flat tyre on his car, he wasn't sure which. He stood watching as he worked the wheel, fingering the blade in his pocket with the familiar current of elation running through his groin, but something in the man's eyes, a coldness, something dead, ran through him, making his fingers retract from the knife's handle. He didn't think the man would go quietly. Sometimes he enjoyed the dance he and his victims did, both physically and mentally, he didn't think he'd find any joy there out in the desert cutting the life out of this stranger.

On the final night of his holiday, while up at the far end of the Strip he'd been mugged. He'd killed a mugger before in Philadelphia, there he'd sensed it coming, saw the thief take him in, mark him as prey, he recognised the signs as his own. He'd loitered in a doorway and then made off slowly between two buildings and stood in the shadows lighting a cigarette while the mugger came in close, something glinting in his hand. He turned to meet him, grabbing the man's wrist suddenly and stubbing the cigarette out on his fingers, the knife clattered to the ground and as he yelled out in surprise and pain, he head-butted him and broke his wrist as he fell to the floor. He hefted the body into a dumpster, covered it with bags and boxes and rejoined the throng on the street who never stopped moving even as he'd throttled the life out of the would-be attacker less than fifty feet away. This time it was different, he'd been near wasteland, ground undergoing development between two of Vegas' oldest hotels on the now unfashionable end of the Strip. The earlier heat had given him a headache and what felt like a touch of sunstroke, he felt sluggish and the constant carnival of lights and sound had driven him away into the dusky reaches of the town as night fell. He'd been touching the back of his neck tentatively, feeling the warmth rising up from his skin when he felt the gun pushing him in the back. There were two of them, one indicating the waste ground to his left with a quick movement of his head. He wasn't even sure where his knife was; he absent-mindedly patted down his pockets until a sudden jab in the ribs sent him sprawling to his knees. One held the gun to his head, the other pulled the wallet from his back pocket and then a hard kick above his eyebrow punctuated the night with pinpricks of light and then he was lying there looking up at the dark green frame of the construction crane looming above him.

Stay down, fucker, someone shouted, but the voice was receding, already lost to the screech and wail of the cars cruising the Strip. He stood with a grunt and brushed the sand and dirt from his jacket, as he walked towards the road the glare of the halogen lights gave him a dusty aura. To the passenger in the passing cab he looked like he was floating slowly towards the street, his hair backlit so it looked like he was going up in flames.

The next morning he stood before the bathroom mirror, tentatively dabbing at the purple and black bloom above his right eye. His arm ached and there was a dull pain above the bridge of his nose like he'd been wearing a tight hat too long. His flight home out of McCarran Airport was booked for later that afternoon; he pulled on a shirt and lifted his jacket with a wince over an outstretched arm. He reached into his inside pocket and fished out his knife, he looked at himself holding it in the mirror and then quickly pocketed it and left. Outside he waved the doorman away and carried his suitcase to the street, hailing a cab as it came racing through the downtown traffic.

Airport, please, he told the driver, holding his stomach and easing himself into the back seat.

Could you, he asked, gesturing to the case sitting on the street. I'm not feeling so great, he said, I'll make it worth your while. The driver loaded his case and slammed the trunk shut, causing the back suspension to buckle momentarily.

You okay? asked the driver, his eyes wide in his rearview mirror as he picked out the bruising above his passenger's eye. Rough night? he asked.

I'm okay, he replied. I just picked up a stomach bug, too much of a good thing, he smiled before indicating his eye. Then I went over in the bathroom, rushing to get in there, you know, he said. The driver smiled an accomplice's smile. They drove on in silence until he doubled up in the back seat and yelped with pain.

You okay? asked the driver again, instinctively slowing down.

I'm alright, he said, grimacing with pain, he clutched at his stomach and let out a low moan, his eyes closing.

Want me to stop? asked the driver almost turning in his seat.

I need some cover, he said. You'll have to get off the highway.

The driver quickly scanned the lanes around him and nosed his way to an off ramp, made a circuit of the loops that criss-crossed the highway until they were facing the way they came, pulled onto a side road and then drove until the stream of cars quietened and shrubs and small trees began to appear at the roadside. The cab rolled to a stop, parking up on the verge, and he scrambled from the back seat and disappeared into the undergrowth. He sat there in the dappled light, enjoying the silence and the shade. He heard the driver's door open and then close.

You alright in there? the cab driver shouted. He grunted noncommittally in return then stood silently, his knife upturned in his hand as if he were preparing to fight. The next time the cab driver called out to him he feigned a terrified scream and he came scrambling through the bushes and onto the point of his blade. The driver gasped and tried to wrest himself away, but he held him by the small of the back like dancers in a clinch and worked the knife up towards his sternum until two folds of skin flopped open and his insides were outside, soaking through his shirt and pushing at the gash in the material and his belly. Sorry, he said as he laid the body onto the grass, pulling it into the shade and out of sight. He fished the car keys from his pocket and moments later he was navigating his way back towards the highway. He pulled into the airport and headed for the long-term parking lot, he found a space that bordered the runway and sat and admired the shape of the planes as they roared into view, casting the cab in fleeting shadows. He changed his shirt, locked the car up and dropped the keys in a bin near the departures lounge and when the girl behind the desk asked him if he'd like an upgrade he said that he would like that very much.

After they'd pulled his mother from the water, they sent for his father to come and get him. They'd divorced the year before, but were still friends as far as he could tell. He remembered his father rushing towards him through the hotel foyer and wrapping him up in his arms, the tears pouring from his already red-rimmed eyes. Later while they were packing her things up his father came across the snowglobe wrapped in tissue paper in the corner of the bag. Did your mother get this? he asked. I don't know, he said, taking the glass ball from him to study the dolphin arching through the air within. Give it a shake, said his father slowly and then he held him as the silver snow fell.

He checked he had everything one last time. A car horn sounded outside and he crossed to the window and waved to the cab driver who was leaning against his car bonnet, with a folded paper underneath one arm. He flicked through the city guide he'd bought for his trip and then dropped it into the side pocket of his case and zipped it shut. He hoisted the smaller bag onto his shoulder and lifted the suitcase with a grunt. He turned to look at his apartment and made his way down the stairs and out to the car, the cab driver took the suitcase from him with two hands and swung it in a half circle into the trunk, it barely made a sound as it slid into place.

You want to hold on to that, he asked, indicating the bag over his shoulder. He nodded and climbed into the car.

Airport, right? said the cab driver.

Yes, please, he replied.

Good to get away, said the cab driver. Yes, it was, he agreed, it always was good to get away.

Chorus

He liked having his father in the car, no matter if he was an apparition or not. He found he'd enjoyed the old man's company on the last few miles of his journey, plus the time and the distance — and how far was eternity anyway? — seemed to have mellowed him. As they'd pulled away from Vegas he had become less rigid, less the father he remembered and more the one he'd sometimes wished for, especially since his death. His father could still flare, but his outbursts were softer now and tempered by concern.

Come home, his father had said. I'm sorry I hurt you.

He didn't have a home to go to any more, but he didn't tell his father that, he guessed he might have known anyhow. The dry brush and sandy earth went past as a green and brown blur. His father was still talking to him.

I was too hard on you as a kid, he said, before something

suddenly attracted his attention to his right, his head swivelling to take it in.

I shouldn't have shut you up in the cellar, his father said. That young girl you had down there, she died, you know. They didn't get to her in time. They'll go through the gardens now, churn up all those beautiful flowers and all the landscaping your mother loved and they'll find the bones, the skulls. His father paused as if trying to control his register and tone. Did you even bury that last guy? You did, didn't you? he asked, his voice began to sound like he was becoming exasperated.

It doesn't matter now, said the driver.

I don't know why you stopped taking them down to the water and dumping the remains off the coast, it wasn't like we didn't have a boat. You got lazy. His father's voice rose angrily and abruptly as he talked and the driver instantly felt uneasy and small, young again. He flinched in anticipation of the impending blow, but it never came. His voice softened again.

I ran around on your mother, you knew, right? His father was dressed in his favourite black suit, his greying hair was parted and neat, he had oil holding it in place. He was nursing his glasses in his lap. He opened the window a little and the cooling air played around his face. He looked down at his father's hands set firmly on his knees. They were as massive as he remembered. He thought about them being around his throat, clenched into cruel fists to strike him. He also remembered them lifting him up when he was a kid, tickling him, dunking him in the sea to the sound of his own excited laughter, and later those arms wrapped around him as he drifted to a soundless sleep in the front seat of the car.

But when she died, when the doctors told me the cancer was terminal, his father said and he was staring out of the window when he said it,

I knew there was no way back then, that I couldn't make it up to her or you in time. That's when I really started with the bottle, drinking all hours of the day and night. I lost the respect of my guys after that. They were talking about getting rid of me, you know? He mimed a handgun going off against the side of his head. *People forget everything you did for them, I guess. Your mother forgave me anything, but not those guys, and I guess I lost you and your sister too.* His father looked at him, but he wouldn't return his gaze.

The car behind him flashed his headlights then sounded its horn and both father and son sat up.

What the fuck? said his father. *You going to take that?* His voice was suddenly broad and threatening again, like the one he used to hear coming up from the kitchen, when his father's friends would stay late and the house smelt of cigar smoke and his father was losing at cards. Eventually he'd fall asleep, floating away to the murmur of voices as they filled the lower part of the house.

He realised that he'd been drifting in traffic while caught up in their conversation, moving far too slow for the regimented speed of the highway, but he was incensed anyway, inflamed by his father's anger and ashamed that his father had found him wanting. He eased back on the accelerator so that he was almost freewheeling and weaved a little to frustrate the driver in the red car behind him. His father laughed approvingly. Passing drivers pulled away from him; looks of irritation crossing their faces. The car behind them flashed him and the horn blared again. His father cocked an eyebrow and he found himself reaching around behind him and underneath his seat for his wrench. He braked suddenly and looked at his father for affirmation, but he couldn't remember if he got it before everything turned red and the anger and desperation were flushing up through him.

★ ★ ★

What have you done, what have you done? screamed his father. He was seated back in the car, everything was still except his heart beating madly against his chest; he imagined it breaking through the layers of skin and bone, then borne into the air and moving out of sight until there was just the sound of it travelling toward the colour-less horizon ahead of him, eventually thrumming into nothing as it rose into the air. He turned to explain to his father what had happened, although he wasn't sure he knew. He was feeling like he was eight years old again, ready to apologise for his mistakes as he had done all his life and then he saw that his father was gone. He looked wildly around, almost expecting to see him sitting in the back seat smiling, ready to clap him hard on the shoulder and let out that familiar laugh, but all that was behind him were people spilling out on to the side of the highway from a roadside diner, a woman collapsing into the arms of a man, someone on their knees was shouting. The tint across the top of his windshield made it look like the sky was darkening.

Dad, he cried out. He sped up trying to catch his father's fleeting ghost, but the highway was empty, all the other cars had crested the hill ahead and moved out of sight. It was just sky and desert waiting up ahead.

Dad, Daddy, he called again, but it was only the sound of the radio that responded.

Song 9: Eat

In the roadside restaurant they were playing Neil Diamond's *Sweet Caroline*. He sat there, fingers thrumming the beat on the table; the restaurant came into life, some patrons loudly singing the horn parts from the song's chorus:

Sweet Caroline! Dah Da Da!

They boomed, slamming their knives and forks on the table-tops to keep time; plastic tomatoes oozing ketchup were suddenly instruments of percussion among the clamour, sugar bowls jumped into life, teaspoons were tapped.

Dah Da Da! Good times never felt so good . . .

Honey, she said.

He was staring out of the window, humming to himself.
Honey?

He looked at the bright blue bouncing off the highway beyond the glass and let the racing cars come into focus and then drift out again, turning to black as they disappeared into the low sun, he felt hot. He liked the sound the cars made; their vibrations flattening out on the slick tarmac and buffeting the windows. He pressed his forehead against the glass to feel their blurring motion as they slid past.

Honey.

Her voice was more urgent now; she placed her hand on his elbow until he turned to look at her.

Eat something, she said.

The table between them was laden with burgers, there were three tall glasses filled with rippled scoops of ice cream, long spoons sat upright in the rounds of chocolate, there were bowls of fries connecting the main courses to the desserts, acting as bridges between meals. Coffee and Coke sat slopping in their respective cups and glasses. Sugar was scattered across the table. Neither of them took sugar, he wondered where it came from.

Ants, he said.

She tilted her head, her hand had moved towards his tightly clenched fist.

The sugar; we'll get ants, he said.

He indicated the table between them helplessly. She held the burger towards him, almost suppliant in her gesture. He took it and bit into it, he realised that no one was singing any more, the radio wasn't even on. A car came in close and he turned to breathe it in, to admire its untroubled passage from window frame to window frame and then out to the horizon.

When he turned back she was sitting with ketchup and crumbs in a ring around her mouth. Her hand was reaching for the sundae. Packets of sweetener were scattered before her torn and empty. The sugar, he thought, looking down, dabbing at the table top and inspecting his glittering fingertip, who takes sugar?

In retrospect, life was a dream before, a dazzling celebration of life, a black sky filled with fireworks every night, it seemed that they were always standing in their yard whooping each explosive plume as the coloured stars tumbled to earth. He was sure that was how he'd felt when the three of them had been together.

The sundae glass was empty and she was tipping it back like a drunk chasing the worm in a bottle of tequila. She caught his eye, placed the glass on the table and grabbed a handful of fries and ate them, washing them down with a gulp of Coke. She leant forward and coughed violently, but waved his hand away as he leant forward to help. They rarely touched any more, their hands sometimes brushed when they were passing food to each other, but they'd shake it away as if there were residue on their skins that might burn if they let it stay too long, like lime. She waved the waitress over and ordered a grilled cheese sandwich, a burger, more coffee and another sundae.

Like Elvis, said the waitress who in spite of herself was staring.

His wife's face was flecked and smeared, ruddy with food, she'd grab at one plate after the next, leaving no space between courses, him clutching the table as if the restaurant might tip violently at any moment and he'd be the only one left holding on. He pushed his head up against the glass, leaving a half moon of sweat and condensation, gawping at the cars like a kid staring up expectantly at a Christmas sky trying to pick out Santa's reindeers. They both stopped to stare at her as she cleared their table, she half expected them to growl sullenly, they looked feral.

On Sundays the three of them used to drive out to the diner for brunch. They'd take the corner booth if it was free, he'd read the paper, glancing up from the supplements, she'd drink coffee and pick at her sandwich, tapping sachet upon sachet of sweetener into her cup, the circular tinkle of her teaspoon the only sound. Their son, Alex, would press himself up against the window, watching the cars go by, his hands leaving sticky imprints on the glass. His mother would pull him down in his seat and point him at his burger that he'd eat while kicking his legs under the table. Sometimes he'd drift out to the tyres hanging on ropes next to the slide and climbing frame at the back of the restaurant and swing listlessly as the midday heat came to bear on his thin shoulders. In the near distance the highway hummed like white noise.

I can't eat another thing, she said as she broke the crust free from her sandwich and pushed it into her mouth. You've hardly eaten anything, she said as they surveyed the debris between them. It looked as though their table had been attacked by a flock of ravenous birds.

That looks like the car, he said, sitting up as the blue Pontiac pulled into the diner's car park.

That car wasn't blue, it was black, she said, though her eyes followed the car as hungrily as his. They watched the man walk from his vehicle to the stool at the counter and only averted their gaze when he turned to meet their curious glances.

It might have been him, he said wearily.

Do you want some doughnuts? she asked, scanning the laminated menu. He nodded mutely. The waitress regarded them coolly, gave her blunted pencil a lick and waited for the woman's hand to once more rise and wave her over.

The driver didn't know how long he'd actually been driving – it felt like days – and he wasn't sure where he was when he crested over the hill and saw the long straight ahead of him. Cars were pulling away from his and disappearing into the distance. He was vaguely aware of the low-lying buildings off to the right up ahead. His head hurt and black dots played in front of his eyes, his stomach gurgled making his breath acidic and stale in his mouth. Someone behind him flashed their headlights and then leant on his horn causing him to sit up in his seat. He'd slowed right down and was weaving a little, unaware of the wheel, his foot idling on the accelerator. The horn blared again, longer this time, he could feel it pulsing through him. He slowed deliberately causing the red Chrysler behind to almost shunt him and then pull wildly to one side to avoid smashing into him. The horn blared again, the Chrysler's headlights flashed.

Fuck you, he sneered, fuck you.

He reached around, looking for something that could double as a weapon, something like a jack or tyre iron, he found himself wishing he still had his gun.

The diner was filling up. It was almost lunchtime. The waitresses moved among the tables, slapping orders down in front of the chef, shouting things he couldn't make out. The sounds of the diners and the hum of the road rushed through his ears and filled his head, it sounded like waves crashing.

Why did he speed up, do you think? Just when he was slowing down, why wouldn't he stop? he asked her.

Eat, she said, spooning ice cream into his mouth. She broke off a piece of doughnut and added that to the next spoonful. She dabbed at his mouth with her napkin. He moved the burger around on his plate, fishing the slice of cheese out then folding it neatly before popping it into his mouth. She beamed at him, happy to see him eat.

The boy was swinging as high as the tyre would let him, the rope creaking back and forth. He sat inside the ring, his hands clasped across the top, holding on to the rope. He dropped his head back and watched his outstretched feet race towards the sky and then fall backward to the ground again. It made him dizzy and he felt the blood creeping into his cheeks and his head get hot. His father came out of the diner and stood watching him for a while, the small figure swooping back and forth, laughing delightedly with each sweeping pass.

You look like Tom Sawyer, he shouted.

The boy turned his head to look at him, his father standing there with one hand on the rail, a foot set tentatively on the first step down to the playground.

Your mother wants to go soon, he called. You going to be okay to go?

Five minutes, he replied, feeling the air coming out of him as his stomach rolled over with each swing.

His father went back in, the glass and chrome door clunking

shut, and he leant back as far as he dared, terrified and exhilarated as the tyre described arcs against the summer sky. He wondered how much it would take to the push the tyre over the crossbar and feel the world fall away as he completed a squealing revolution through the air. He was slowing down – his rising and falling dwindling in both urgency and power – when he heard the squealing of brakes and the angry stabs of car horns coming from the road beyond the squat diner. The sound rose like smoke into the air.

The plate between them was empty, broken circles of grease glimmered dully like a faded pattern on its surface. They were both licking their fingers, almost happily.

Good doughnuts, she said. He nodded, holding his coffee cup with both hands. This was the closest they'd come to happiness since the accident, times like these when they were sated, felt safe and achingly full. Their couples therapist – they'd both strained to escape each other as soon as they started seeing their sadness reflected in the other's face, but had fought against the urge to flee – had told them they might never heal. They found drinking and the deep comfort of food helped them feel otherworldly or numb, each was easier to deal with than themselves. It was like coming back here to the diner in the hope that one day the images flickering beyond the window might rewrite themselves and still their trembling world and stop the creeping blackness that brought them roaring awake at night, raging against their dreams and memories, screaming and tearful.

The driver pulled his Lexus across the highway, his head was thumping, his heart racing, he placed a hand against his chest and tried to still the beating. He pushed at the door with a grunt, righted himself with an unsteady hand, walked to the rear of his car and kicked at the trunk, the lid popping open with a slow hiss, and grabbed a wrench from inside. The red car that had flashed him backed up slowly as the driver, confusion and fear in his eyes, tried to manoeuvre his vehicle past and escape the madman raging and cursing in the middle of the highway, straddling the yellow line that divided the road. The driver, the wrench clenched tightly in his hand, was shouting something, as he came in close his white vest was streaked with dirt, ribs pushing through the cotton, his hair matted and standing on end, there was a mask of sweat on his face. He paused for a moment, pushing the wrench down into the waistband at the back of his jeans, and placed both palms lightly on the car bonnet.

I don't know what your fucking problem is, he said to the silhouetted figure before him. It was hard to make out his features with the sunlight casting a white blur across the windscreen.

His voice was low and tired as he said it, his face jutting forward, his features sharp yet emaciated like the prow of a once glorious ship now dry docked and running to rust. Why you're honking your horn at me . . . His voice trailed away and he gulped, trying to force back the tears that were gathering in his eyes.

Firstly he took the knife from his pocket and placed it under the winged Chrysler logo on the car's grille, working it back and forth until it slowly pulled away and came off in his hand. He held it up by its tip for the man in the red car to see and then jammed it in to the waist of his jeans like it was some kind of trophy. Then he pulled the wrench from behind his back, held it high above his head in both hands and then he brought it down hard on the bonnet, flecks of red paint thrown up by the impact, he did it again, two, three times.

You're fucking nuts, the man in the car screamed. Though he was checking that all his doors and windows were locked while he said it, then reversing quickly back he hit the car idling behind him in the traffic that had slowly built up. He heard his brake lights shatter as the thin figure stood before him swinging the steel cross above his head. More cars slowed at the crest of the hill, the cacophony of horns at odds with the still, dusty landscape. The driver of the Lexus dropped the silver wrench and let it bounce away from him, then he caught the eye of the driver whose car he'd just attacked, saw that he was sitting as far back in his seat as he could as if the extra inches might save him if the wrench came crashing through the glass. His eyes were wide, he was clinging to his seat belt even though he was stationary, his knuckles white with fear. Then the shambling figure in the white vest, disconsolate, teary and hopeless, straightened up, stared balefully at the train of cars that had now come to a halt behind his and climbed back into the driver's seat and gunned the engine into life.

He let the car idle and sat there fiddling with the radio dial, slumped in his seat; there were dots of dried paint on his arms. The sound of revving engines and car horns built as cars slowly started pulling around him. He gave some stranger the finger as he pulled up alongside him to shout something. All he saw was the disconnected anger lining the stranger's face. A classic rock station broke through the static of the radio and he sat there tapping his leg distractedly. Most of the traffic had cleared, but cars kept racing up to the crest of the hill and seeing his car parked across the road pulled wildly to one side and pressed on their horns as they went snaking past, the back wheels seeking purchase on the blacktop as they slid wildly sideways before regaining their line.

From the playground it sounded as though a race had started on the highway. The boy stepped down from the tyre; it twirled slowly as he walked towards the road kicking a pebble before him. He came up past the restaurant, inside he could just make out the shape of his parents, his father hidden behind his newspaper, his mother's hand on the teaspoon in her cup; she was looking out of the window as if the noise had caught her attention too. He picked at the sesame seed between his teeth and looked out at the two cars, one red, one black, racing side by side down the highway. His mother saw them too and pulled gently at his father's newspaper.

Where's Alex? she asked.

Out the back, swinging on a tyre, said his father, he's playing, he's okay. His eyes hadn't left the page, he was holding on to a sentence, eager not to lose his place.

Back behind the wheel, the driver pulled away and began to breathe deeply like his therapist had shown him. He felt the air expanding in his chest as it came through the open window and his heart began to settle, he brushed the paint from his arms and then was suddenly thrown sideways as the car that had pulled up next to him, clipped his wing, paint cracked, the violent collision tearing his rearview mirror off. It spun into the air, the chrome catching the light and disappearing over his head. The driver of the Chrysler was a few feet away from him, screaming at him. The car came in close again and he steeled himself for the impact, his hands gripping the wheel.

His father was reading the paper, his mother standing in the playground at the rear of the restaurant gently pushing the empty tyre, calling his name. It was hot, she could feel the dust in her throat, she called out again. Then something happened behind her, a sound came from the road, something out of sight but forever in view.

He felt the car sliding out from under him, drifting almost peacefully to one side, the tarmac beneath him turned to sand and loose stones, the driver who had shunted him leant on his horn and sped away. He saw the diner rise up quickly before him and then a small blonde figure appeared and then was snatched away, folding in on itself and then gone.

The boy rolled in time with the wheels, spinning briefly in synchronicity and then bumped beneath the speeding car's body and was finally thrown out wildly like branches from a thresher, his body skipping along the surface of the highway, his T-shirt torn from him, one arm across his face as if shading his eyes from the sun. He slid to a halt in the sandy dirt at the side of the road, his small, broken frame raising a cloud of dust.

The driver felt something rattling beneath his feet and then just the rhythmic roll of the highway again as he regained control of the car and slowed as people rushed from the diner. Commotion, he muttered and pressed down hard on the accelerator, rushing towards the burning sun that waited for him beyond the ribbon of road he was on.

It was dusk by the time they got home; he wiped the crumbs from his shirt as they exited their car. Good lunch, he said, tugging at his ever-tightening waistband. They stood at the top of the stairs and looked in at their son's room, he walked in and sat on the bed and felt the hot flush of tears on his face. He held the pillow up to his face and imagined his son's scent there. He lay there with the pillow pulled up against him and remembered the mornings when he came in here and gently roused his son from his sleep, leaning down to kiss the straw–coloured crown of his head.

The sound of the shower came into life across the hallway. He stood up and crossed the room, placing the pillow back on the bed. He looked back at his son's room and quietly closed the door. He walked into the bathroom, admiring his wife's form wreathed in steam in the shower. The scars ran along her back and at her sides as if she'd been clawed by a wild animal. She sensed him there and turned to smile at him, her hair slick and brushed back from her face. He took off his shirt, the scars along his paunchy torso mirroring hers. He undressed and stood under the hot water next to her, both of them turning red, two mute embers standing side by side.

He sat in the living room in his robe, flicking listlessly between television channels. His wife came in, a towel wrapped around her; on one side, stark against the white cotton, was a small red bloom, she held something gently in her palm.

You should eat, she said, arm extended towards him.

He took the sliver of bloody flesh from her and placed it on his tongue and then quickly swallowed it. He undid his robe and took the knife from the table next to him and grabbed at the loose skin of his stomach.

Stop, she said, and he looked up at her, surprised.

She leant forward with the corner of the towel and dabbed at the blood around his lips. You made a mess, she said and then tightened the towel around her and waited for him to finish.

Chorus

The driver sat heavily down on the floor with a sigh. Despite the desert heat he pulled his shirt off and started wiping away the blood from the front of his Lexus. The grille was sticky with it and the headlight was red like a stop sign. He sat in the shade cast by his car and rested his head back against the door. He was parked up on a side road away from the highway, though he could hear it calling him over the low, dusty hills. He knew he'd have to ditch the car, but he was out here alone and he needed to keep moving, he was sure the police would want to talk to him about the boxes he'd left behind in Jersey and he'd hit something on the highway and he hadn't stopped. He still hoped his father would reappear in the car's passenger seat and help him to understand what was fact and what was fiction. He was still covered in flakes of dry paint and the Chrysler logo sat in the sand next to him. He picked it up and twirled it between his fingers in order to watch it catch the light and then he stood up walked back beyond the car towards the brow of the nearest hill and threw it as far as he could into the scrub.

When he turned to walk back, there was a police car parked next to his. It sat strangely mute, its lights pulsing in slowly drifting red circles. He was still holding the bloody shirt in his hand and he tightened his fingers around it to conceal the stains. The patrolman was squatting down examining the car's grille; he stood and turned as the driver came down the slope towards him.

You'll burn, said the patrolman, indicating the shirt in the driver's hand. He was standing very straight with one hand placed on his gun holster. He hadn't popped the button that opened it, but the driver knew it was only a matter of time.

Where you headed? asked the patrolman.

The coast, he said.

Family? asked the patrolman.

My father's out there, said the driver and for a moment he believed it himself. That he'd get out to the water and his father would be standing there on a white sand beach in shorts and a polo shirt waving him home as the sun was setting.

What brings you out here? Why'd you stop? said the patrolman, who was examining the dent in the bumper of the Lexus.

Got tired, he said. I just pulled off the road to sleep, I've been on the road for days. He indicated the generous back seat as if he'd only just woken there moments before.

What were you doing up there? said the patrolman and looked over at the slope that the driver had just descended.

Call of nature, smiled the driver. No law against it, right?

Not out here, I guess, said the patrolman. Got your paperwork? he said, his tone suddenly businesslike and brusque. The driver reached into the car and rooted around in his glove compartment while the

Lexus pinged its annoyance at the open door. The patrolman stood very close to him, just beyond his shoulder. He turned around with his licence and registration in his hand and noticed the patrolman's holster was open. The patrolman took the papers from him and walked towards his car. Then he stopped and turned and looked at the driver and then down at the shirt clenched in his fist.

Why don't you put that on? said the patrolman. You'll be all blisters by tomorrow otherwise.

I'm good, said the driver, his free hand shading his eyes. I could do with some colour.

The patrolman was impassive behind his sunglasses, their dark green tint hiding his eyes.

Put it on, said the patrolman and he reached for his holster. The driver ran forward and threw the shirt into the patrolman's face, reaching for the knife in his back pocket as he lunged. The patrolman swept the shirt aside with a gasp, taking a step back as he did so; his hand was on his holster when the driver plunged the blade down into his fingers, catching the bone of his knuckle. The patrolman screamed and tried to step back, but the driver held him with his free hand and drew him closer as they fell backwards, driving his head into his face. They bounced off the bonnet of the patrol car and fell apart, the driver scrambling to his feet first, knife to hand, kicking his boot heel at the patrolman's wounded hand, causing the patrolman to reach across with his free hand to protect it and as he did so the driver forced the blade into the side of his neck. It went up to the hilt and he stepped back as the patrolman reached for the handle, his feet shuffling in the sand. He gasped again and blood gathered at his lips, then he shuddered as if he'd felt a sudden chill and was still. The driver pulled the knife from his neck and pulled the body up and over his shoulder. The blood from the wound ran down his bare back and into the waistband of his jeans. He removed the patrolman's shirt even though it had blood smeared over the shoulder and his gun and manoeuvred the body into the Lexus' trunk and then leant against the back of his car and lit a cigarette. His breath was coming in short, hard spurts and he felt sticky and his shoulders burnt. He drove the Lexus up over the hill where he'd tossed the Chrysler logo, parked it out of sight and walked back to the patrol car. The radio was chattering with life so he turned it off and sat down in the driver's seat. He found the keys still in the ignition, grabbed them and went to the trunk. It sprang open to reveal a high powered rifle and a clip of bullets, what looked like black army fatigues, two bottles of water and a nightstick. He bounced the latter against the ground and grinned as the telescopic arm shot out. Ha! He shouted, striking the sand repeatedly. Ha! Then he took the bloody shirt he'd been wearing, siphoned some gas from his own tank, soaked the top and walked back towards his car. He laid it on the back seat of the Lexus and built a small impromptu fire out of old unpaid parking tickets and scraps of paper next to the armrest. He threw his licence on top, knowing that he wouldn't need it again now. He lit the paper and whispered and blew onto the shirt, encouraging it to take as it smouldered indecisively. By the time he walked away from the car, black smoke was filling the back seat and he could smell the leather seats starting to burn. He hoped it would explode in a plume of smoke and flames before he'd driven too far away so that he could enjoy the show. He pushed the patrolman's shades on to his nose and pulled on his bloodied shirt. It was too big for his slight frame, but he tucked it in as tightly as it would go, sniffing at the blood on the shoulder as he made his way towards the patrol car.

He pulled back onto the highway and started to enjoy the impact he made; how oncoming cars slowed when they saw him approaching.

He hit his lights a few times and drove past laughing when cars pulled over to stop. He made threatening gestures to a few drivers, wagging his finger sternly and enjoying the perplexed look on their faces. He hit his sirens briefly too and watched startled figures in front of him jump in their seats. They'd drift to the far lane and he'd gun his engine and sail past. He tried the lights and the siren and floored the accelerator as if chasing an adversary, watching happily as the traffic before him opened up like a theatre curtain. When he'd had enough of the game, he pulled off the highway and headed to the baked-looking hills that overlooked the road. He parked up the car and examined the patrolman's rifle. He had his revolver strapped to his hip, but he guessed the rifle was anything but regulation issue. It was a high-powered hunting rifle with a telescopic sight, the kind he remembered from watching the high-flyers hunt when he worked his summers in the Canadian resort.

Weekend Warrior cop, he muttered to himself. He found a vantage point to rest the barrel of the rifle on and lay down to survey the valley below through the powerful sight. It was quiet and he traced the silent cars below with the gun and imagined picking off the people below and watching the cars racing wildly out of control and into the steel barriers and concrete walls. It always amazed him, the carnage one bullet could bring. Then he saw a black Lexus racing through the traffic, its windows tinted, and he wondered briefly if someone had got to his car, smothered the flames and driven it away. He felt a stab of anger that someone might have stolen his car and his finger tightened on the trigger, and then he saw the patrol cars racing in its wake. The traffic up ahead was being pulled over and then the Lexus swerved wildly to one side, left the ground briefly – he saw sunlight and shadow on the road beneath its wheels – and hit the far wall, its wing crumpling on impact, it spun once and then stopped. The police appeared suddenly and yanked a man from the Lexus and threw him to the floor. He thrashed around as they tried to handcuff him, he was screaming something and one of the cops hit him with an open hand that flattened him back onto the tarmac. It was then that the driver realised that they thought it was him that they'd apprehended down on the highway. He looked at the black Lexus and back at the slowly inching traffic and then he started shooting.

Song 10: Bride

Her name was Sylvia and she twinkled back at him from her online picture. He read her profile, taking in every detail; she was born in Verkhoturye (when he tried to pronounce it out loud he couldn't help but add three or four extra consonants – it sounded like he was taking a long and complicated sneeze). The Russian Brides site said she was twenty-four, though he guessed she might be closer to thirty given the lines around her eyes and smile. She was a Pisces; he didn't know what that meant, but his dead wife had been a Pisces so he took that as a positive sign, some sort of approving nod from beyond the grave. She liked to travel and she liked herring. He had never eaten any and so bought some the first chance he got, tightly coiled in a jar, rolling around in a yellow mayonnaise sauce. He picked it gingerly out of its glass container and marvelled at its yielding, soft flesh. It was oily and raw-tasting, he briefly imagined it being yanked from the sea and held aloft, its flapping body slowing to meet its fate. He wrinkled his nose at the smell and its salty flesh, but ate it determinedly with his eyes closed as if that might ward off the taste and smell. The next time he wrote to her he made sure that he let her know that he liked herring too. At night, he'd trace her background and history over the internet; her town, the oldest in the South Ural region (when he said it he made it rhyme confidently with plural) had been cut off from the West for years, a shady military complex with huge mineralogical deposits, it had been an area for weaponry development and, he surmised from his research, a tough place to bring up children. Even the nearby monastery was inexplicably and heavily fortified while one of the biggest tourist attractions was a Museum of Nuclear Weapons. There was also a place where you could discover how the Russians developed the machinery for chemical warfare during the Cold War. He imagined Sylvia as a strident fiery bloom growing among the weeds of her empire's past. Before Russian Brides he'd written to women in a prison in Indiana, his friend had suggested it, and once he'd got past the names they'd adopted for their online profiles; Priestess, Black Widow, The Kat – he felt like he were writing to a biker gang – he began to enjoy their correspondence. Sometimes, the letters would be censored by black marker pen and he was dismayed when he found that Priestess, real name Penny (grand larceny, attempted manslaughter, affray), had added five years to her sentence when she'd attacked a prison guard in the laundry room with a sharpened clothes peg. He couldn't believe it, and fretted nervously the first time they'd talked on the phone (she was allowed one call a week as part of her privileges) as she told him that she'd kill for him if he'd wait for her. He sat mutely at home, the shadows lengthening across his living room and marvelled at the clanging of steel gates and the clamour of voices in the background that sometimes threatened to swamp her words. He'd thought of travelling to the heart of Indiana to the penitentiary set in its own acres of dry grassland, surrounded by floodlights and observation towers with their armed guards (he'd seen it online). To walk through the shuddering iron gates, each one closing noisily behind him, and into a room partitioned by a glass wall and small booths, set with their own red phones. He imagined his palm pressed against the glass, mirroring Priestess' actions across from him, both setting their phones forlornly down as the guard called time on the visiting session. Later he realised that all the images he'd imagined were drawn from films and TV dramas he'd seen, he had no idea of what the real interior of a prison might look like. He finally let those letters quietly drop but still panicked when an official-looking letter with the prison service crest came through the door. He imagined looking up and seeing the Black Widow standing in his garden, waving before breaking her way in to exact revenge for all the letters he'd promised but never sent. He was ashamed to admit he felt a thrill at the thought.

Russian Brides was easier, these were women on a different continent, and none, as far as he knew, had ever stolen a car from outside a Walgreens so that they could try to rob a store with a starting pistol. He didn't even think they had branches of Walgreens in Russia. Sylvia looked almost demure, but had promise and he was sure she'd never sharpen a clothes peg and stick it in someone's thigh, at least not without good reason. A friend asked him if he knew that all those Russian dating sites were run by the Russian mob and that most of the girls were under the cosh of organised crime. He had to ask him what cosh meant, but he knew it was nothing good. The next time he wrote to Sylvia he asked if she was in trouble, and if she was labouring under an unforgiving regime and she replied that it was no more unforgiving that the one she'd grown up with. He was confused and couldn't tell if she was joking or not. Is there anything you want to tell me, he wrote and could hear his voice hissing in his head as if not to be overheard in some way. Only that I like your eyes, she responded and her connection to the machinations of the Russian underground were never mentioned again.

To reach Verkhoturye he had to fly into Ekaterinburg (Ural's buzzing capital, as the guidebooks described it), via Moscow. By the time he'd landed he felt as though he'd been in the air for days and the staunch pain in his lower back made him wonder if the hostess had kicked him while he'd slept. He perused his guidebook as the plane emptied, alighting on the words, buzzing and metropolis, though very little appeared to be moving outside his window. Sylvia, her mother and a man who remained ominously silent met him at the airport. It was early autumn and bitterly cold and Sylvia and her mother were pale, unreadable faces swathed in hats and scarves. His coat flapped uselessly about him as they crossed the tarmac and his eyes streamed in the unremitting wind. Over the next few days he discovered that it was not only the monastery but the cathedral that was fortified too. He tried making a joke about both iconic buildings being two of the most heavily defended sanctuaries he'd ever seen, though Sylvia only looked confused and the quiet man just stared at him with contempt. He saw numerous caves and lakes, he spent an afternoon at Zone No. 145 where the Russians developed their nuclear weapons and one day even travelled five kilometres out of town to bear witness to a memorial dedicated to the slain victims of Stalin's repression (this was translated to him loudly from the grand-looking brass plate by Sylvia). All things considered, he thought, he couldn't blame Sylvia for wanting to leave her home. The fauna, as predicted, was fulsome and startling, as were most of the two hundred national parks throughout South Ural (he felt like he saw them all), but it wasn't enough to tie you to a place made infamous as the valley where the former Soviet Union conceived their weapons of mass destruction. And the wind, he thought, as his hair fell into his eyes for the thousandth time, the wind was inhuman.

They called it a dowry, but it was really a fee, a price tag that he paid for Sylvia, and even while they celebrated with caustic-tasting wine and cake hard enough to knock a stranger out if you'd lobbed it into a crowd, he found himself feeling dirty and tragic that it had come to this. He stepped outside and looked on the ruddy beauty of the valley he was standing in, the distant shimmer of a lake could sometimes be glimpsed like a promise. Evening was falling and tomorrow he would return to California and wait for Sylvia to come to banish the shadows that haunted him, take away the crippling fear and loss in his guts. She joined him on the steps of her house as her mother and the ever-silent man worried the curtain to stand in the window behind them and watch their every move. She linked an arm through his and he wondered why he'd come all this way to a place he could neither spell nor say to find hope in a face he'd found peeking out of his computer monitor so many months before.

Are you happy, she asked him, and all he could do was nod as he tasted the tears that had reached his mouth.

It had been over two years since he woke up in his chair and knew that she'd gone. He tried to stay sleeping to stave off the inevitable realisation like a child who hides its eyes and tells you that you can't see them because they can't see you. He couldn't explain it, but he knew the knock at the door was a policeman and he knew that the policeman would be crying. His neighbour was standing with the policeman; he looked like he'd been punched hard in the stomach by circumstance.

It's Lulu, said his neighbour, but he already knew that too. He let the policeman in and his neighbour too, but his neighbour loitered by the living room door and quietly let himself out with a nod before the policeman had finished speaking.

I'm sorry, said the policeman. He believed he was too.

There was a shooting out on the highway, the policeman said.

He nodded mutely, had someone shot his wife? Why would someone shoot Lulu?

We were chasing a suspect, we were chasing his car, we think he ran a small boy down and didn't stop.

He was numb; someone had run a child down and not stopped? He wondered where their son Charlie was and if he was safe, but Charlie was away in college miles from here. The policeman was still talking to him; he seemed lost in his own thoughts.

We chased the car down, he said, we chased him for miles, he was out of control and then when we managed to stop him, we blew his tyres out, we ran a strip of spikes across the road, it wasn't him. It was the wrong car, it wasn't the man we were after, it was some guy, he was drunk or on dust or something, he was insane, screaming and shouting and as we corralled him with our cars and got him down someone started firing at us from a long way off, up on the hills some place. Someone with a high-powered rifle, we think, someone who knew what he was doing.

The policeman had a cut from shaving just underneath his chin that he worried absently with his right hand.

We don't know who he was, the policeman said. He fired on us and then he started firing on the cars that were passing us so they'd crash into us, we think, that they'd pile up and cause a commotion . . .

Did he get away?

The policeman shrugged helplessly.

He imagined Lulu in her green Impala slowing down as the traffic built up before her and the police lights flashed red and blue in the anaemic Californian sky. He could see the policeman waving the traffic down, slowing the snaking cars as they pulled their suspect to the ground. People were rubbernecking, gawking as the man disappeared beneath a brace of police bodies like prey being pulled down by a pack of lions. The cop waving down traffic swatted suddenly at his shoulder as if he'd been stung and then thrown violently to one side as the blood bloomed through his shirt and his eyes got wide. Then Lulu in her car hearing the sound of the bullets, high and whining as car windows started to shatter and the policemen fell to the floor, their legs kicking out like dogs dreaming, screams and orders being shouted at the same time, someone shunting into her as her car engine roared and then whined and then more bullets thudding noisily into the bodywork, the paint popping off in thick silver and green buttons. A bullet crashing through her window and she felt foolish for jumping as the window cracked and then the next shot hitting her in the neck and her car swerving into the nearest police car, setting off its siren in a lazy, droning wail. More shots ringing out and then there was just the sound of panic and terror filling the air. Some cars sliding almost lazily into the back of those already piled up, adding to the broken jigsaw of vehicles that were spread unevenly across the highway. Then the noise subsiding and smoke spreading through the air and towards the distant hills, leaving only the wailing of urgent sirens distilling the slowly undulating Californian air.

The policeman sat silently across from him, a notepad set on his knee. He fished a card out of his top pocket and handed it across to him, it had a number and his name printed on it in bold black ink. He let himself out as his neighbour let himself back in and stood gingerly over him.

Lulu, he said and let himself be held as emptiness rushed through him and took the strength in his arms and legs away and made him momentarily blind.

There was a photo of her coffin being carried to the grave in the papers, the dead policeman too, his was wrapped in an American flag, they'd been buried miles apart but it had been on the same warm afternoon. Guns saluted his descent into the earth, dirt peppering the lid of the casket sounded hers. Charlie and his girlfriend were there, his neighbours, Lulu's stepmother too and in the distance someone shooting at them but this time with a camera. He went to counselling after Charlie had stayed as long as he could. He couldn't believe that he had to go on alone, that she wouldn't be in the next room when he entered it, he sat up late at night with a blunt-looking revolver before him on the nest of tables, other nights he nursed a bottle of unopened whisky as boxes of painkillers sat strewn on the shelf next to framed portraits of her passing through her unimaginably short life. They were props though; he was magnifying his situation, trying to create a scenario he imagined a widower might need to go through. His pain was real but it was so all-encompassing and unwieldy that he had no idea how to deal with it. He had a very real ache in his shoulders and neck for months that a psychologist insisted was imagined and a symptom of his grief and anguish, but regard-less of the diagnosis he'd still wake each day by sitting up and wincing as the pain rattled through him like old coins in a tin can.

He started online dating at a friend's insistence, but balked at the idea of going out and meeting other people, he'd barely left the house for weeks as it was, only yielding to the pleas of his neighbour to at least take a walk when the weather became unbearably hot and even the full icy impact of his air conditioning couldn't disguise the welcome of the glimmering world outside. If he didn't enjoy the actual idea of dating he did begin to welcome the attention of the people he met on the internet. It would start with emails and in one or two cases instant messaging conversations that went on late into the night. It reminded him of Lulu and the evenings they'd sit together and listen to mixes of music that they'd made each other. They'd applaud the other, sometimes playfully, or coo over a choice the other had made that had significant relevance for them both. He found the Women in Prison website late one night when he couldn't sleep and at first presumed it was porn, but was touched by the testimonials from the inmates on the site looking for someone to write to. Then one morning when the day's new light had brought him around in the same chair again he decided to dedicate himself to a new wife, to blot out the past as much as he could. He couldn't kill himself and he couldn't go on so instead he chose an indifferent middle where he could idle, and for that he'd need someone he neither loved nor hated, but would be around as long as he needed and act as a buffer between him and the wounded, desperate world he now found himself in. That was when he found Russian Brides and Sylvia. Charlie objected, worried that his father's grief had driven him mad, and no matter how many times he explained it to his son, he couldn't believe this temporary state, this sticking plaster, could be what his father truly wanted.

It isn't, he told Charlie, but it's all there is.

He went to the airport to meet Sylvia and her mother who'd be living with them for the first month until her daughter settled in to her new surroundings. He studied the Arrivals board and saw that their plane had landed early and as he stood in the main hall he saw them and their trolley piled high with suitcases before they saw him. He stepped back into an alcove and out of sight as they came closer, offered up a silent prayer to Lulu, tried to rub the redness out of his eyes and then he sprang forward, arms held wide and smiling as his new wife quickened her pace to meet him across the polished white floor.

Chorus

His father had caught him with one of his magazines when he was thirteen. He'd been staring at it transfixed in his room, but privacy wasn't an issue to his father.

My house, he used to say going through every door like it was a challenge.

What the fuck is this? his dad demanded, snatching the issue of Girls, Girls, Girls from his hands and holding it up to the light as if the transparency of the page might give something away, like the watermark on a dollar bill did. His father held his pose for a moment and then his eyes focused in on something on the page. He touched the spot on the page gently with his finger and then withdrew it slowly.

Cute, he said. Where did you get this? There was a pause and then his father spoke again. One of mine, yeah? He sat down next to him on his bed without waiting for an answer.

I'd have shown you this stuff if you said you wanted to see it, he said, but don't go sneaking around in my things, you never know what you might find. He stood up and then paused at the door. Don't tell your mother, he said and threw the magazine at him, causing it to bounce off his chest and spill out across the floor.

Hands! shouted his father as he retreated down the hall, you took your eye off it, hands!

Every time the driver turned the police radio on there was one emergency after another being dispatched. When he listened more closely, ignoring the constant calls coming over the air for him, he realised it was just one emergency: the pile-up on the highway, his pile-up on the highway. They were talking about the shooting and its aftermath. He was staying off the main roads momentarily, but he could still hear the constant whirr of helicopters passing overhead, racing back towards the vehicles and bodies he'd left strewn across three lanes. Ambulance and police sirens wailed in the distance and he wondered how many were dead. He was sure he'd done for a handful of drivers and their passengers, but he wasn't so sure about how many policemen he'd killed. Not even the first one he'd got in the shoulder. It was a very powerful rifle, though; he imagined the impact would have caused massive trauma and damage, surely enough to kill him. He thought about the bullet zigzagging through the policeman's body, ricocheting from bone to bone before exiting in a cloud of red smoke. He was, however, disappointed to note that the shot hadn't even knocked his sunglasses off his stupid fucking head. The police got out of the way pretty quickly, he thought, leaving all those people, all those taxpayers, out there unprotected in their cars. To serve and protect, he thought, to serve and fucking protect.

★　★　★

After that first morning, his father started leaving magazines for him to look at. He'd come in from school and find one had been pushed under his bedroom door or thrown on his bed. He felt excited and dismayed, thrilled to be getting the magazines, but wounded that his father was the one providing them. The initial elation tempered by guilt and the thought that his father might have leafed through them first. He kept thinking about the way his father's face had changed when he had been holding the centrefold up to the window, the concentration on his face. He kept them though. He'd soon filled a shoebox that he kept at the back of his cupboard covered in spare bedding. Intermittently, battered magazines would circulate around school and then disappear again just as abruptly and while friends mourned the limited material available, he was cultivating his own private collection.

He was sitting in the kitchen looking out at the garden when his father came in.

How you doing? his dad asked him. You like that stuff I gave you? It doing it for you? he said, opening the fridge door and looking inside.

He could barely bring himself to speak to his father about it, it's okay, he said, you know.

It's okay, his father boomed. Hey, if that's good enough for me and my guys then what do you need to worry about. Hey, he smiled, you ain't kinky, he paused for effect, or queer?

The boy started to remonstrate, panicking, his cheeks flushed and hot, but his father was laughing, he slammed the fridge door shut and walked over to him with slices of ham folded up in his fingers, he rolled them up and mimed smoking the greasy tube with a smile, swallowed it in one gulp and then he patted his son good naturedly on the knee.

Listen, he said, when that stuff comes in, I grab a copy for you and one for me. I'm sure we both get a kick out of it. I was a kid once, I know how it goes.

He blushed furiously as his father spoke, staring determinedly out of the window.

Now keep it down. Here's your mother, his father said. And as his mother entered the kitchen his father stood and told her he was making coffee and then asked if she'd like some.

He had just turned fourteen when his father asked him if he wanted to see where he worked some nights.

Sure, he said, rising quickly from his bed. It was Friday night and papers and books covered the blankets. His father stopped him with a hand on his chest.

That your homework? he asked.

It's done, he said, I swear. His dad raised his hand as if he might strike him and then dropped it slowly with a smile. You'd better, he said, or she'll have my balls.

Ma won't mind, he started to say, but his father placed a finger at his lips. Shush, he said, let's go get the car.

The strip club sat under the highway. It looked like it might have fallen from the sky, its neon façade blinking in the darkness. It was still, the only sound coming from the cars rushing by overhead, though its parking lot looked busy, down the street he could just make out the lights coming from another bar, hear the faint sound of music when the door swung open, and then it looked like wasteland beyond, the kind of place you'd go to dump unwanted furniture or family pets.

You come here? he asked his father as they exited the car, unable to hide the surprise in his voice. He knew he led an unconventional life, but when he thought of his father at work he was seated in a corner office high in the air, the city a grid of streets far below.

His father looked at him squarely. What do you think pays for your fancy school? he said. Then he laughed. One day this will all be yours, he said, gesturing dramatically, and pushed him towards the entrance with a fist at the small of his back. His father looked immaculate in a pressed black suit and tie, his hair glistening and kept in place with a sheen of oil. As they pushed through the tables to the bar a man stopped his father and looking him up and down asked him whose funeral he was going to. Yours, his father said without missing a beat, you got a problem with that? and then they both fell against each other laughing.

You met my kid? his father asked the man and he didn't hear the reply, but the man smiled and shook his hand vigorously. He was slapped on the back a lot after that and even though his father insisted he drink soda, strangers kept buying him beers and he stood at one end of the bar and drank some of them. His father came and stood next to him and brought him a stool.

Sit there, kid, he said. You enjoying the show? He said he was and they both looked towards the girls dancing up on the small stage across from the bar. They watched, heads nodding softly in time with the music and then he noticed the girl looking across the bar at his father and then at him. She waved and his father waved back and as she moved through the tables towards them he hurried forward to meet her halfway and then he took her by the elbow and turned her around and they navigated their way towards the door next to the stage that led through to the back. His father's head was very close to hers as if he were whispering something in her ear and when the light picked them out as a silhouette the driver thought they looked very much like the Siamese twins he'd seen in his schoolbook.

The girls were naked or very nearly, you never had to wait long and when the first one tore her thong off and whirled it around her head he'd felt himself turn red and had to quickly duck down behind his beer, cooling his cheeks against the cold glass. He was sure his father's friends had noticed or guessed at his discomfort and their laughter was aimed at him, but when he caught the attention of the man who had first shaken his hand, he simply toasted him with his drink and then indicated the girls onstage with a nod and winked. He mouthed, *you okay?* at him and when he motioned that he was, the man touched the barman on the elbow and sent another drink across.

His father was back at his side when the girl the boy had seen across the bar appeared on stage. On her head was a cowboy hat that kept catching the light in broad flashes. As she danced she used it to collect bills from the crowd of men gathered at the front of the stage, inverting it with a shimmy and a smile as it filled up with dollars. His father's friends cheered lustily when she appeared and when he looked at his dad he just grinned and placed a hand on his shoulder. His father had one of his men drive him home that night and when he got back the house was dark and it looked deserted. He lay in bed as the room swirled around him and thought about the girl in the cowboy hat and how he couldn't wait to go back there again.

The driver sat at the side of the road with one door open, his legs propped up on the kerb, he was smoking a cigarette and enjoying the way the sun felt on the back of his neck. He'd put the patrol car's lights on, setting them to a considered revolve, enjoying the dappling light they gave off. He listened to the cars slow as they passed, the oncoming drivers spotting his car and sensing an emergency, then killing their speed accordingly. He stayed out of sight, sat low on the seat and flicked cigarette butts into the field beyond. He wondered where his father was, but didn't think he was coming back anytime soon. He'd disappeared over Christmas one year, suddenly gone from their lives a few days before. He'd been all over the papers, he remembered the detectives at their door, the uniformed men marching through their living room, someone shouting that they had a warrant and that everyone needed to stand back. They went through everything including his presents that sat wrapped under the tree.

Sorry kid, said one officer as he tore at the paper only to find a board game.

Bet you feel fucking clever now, he said to the cop, trying to use his father's voice, but he was intimidated by all the police in his home and was glad when his mother pulled him back behind her and told him to be quiet. They turned everything over and found nothing and spoke quietly and intently to his mother in the kitchen until the family lawyer pulled up sharply in the driveway and came tearing through the house, his coat making an exaggerated shape behind him. He held his briefcase up high as if to ward off evil.

Excuse me, officer, he said to the detective talking to his mother. My client, he snapped and led her back into the living room and stood silently next to her like a sentinel, his eyes trained on the policemen working methodically through room after room.

It's Christmas, he said at one point and picked up the opened presents. Not the kid's stuff too. Don't you people have families? he asked, but he was calm when he said it. You'd better find something, he said and one of the detectives turned to look at him.

We will, he said and rankled as the lawyer made a snorting sound. They didn't though. His father appeared at his bedroom door one night in the listless week between Christmas and New Year.

Miss your old man? he asked, the familiar grin playing on his lips. Come downstairs and say hello to the guys.

Where were you? he asked.

You know better than not to ask that, his father said. Anyway, I was around, I was watching over you. Sorry I missed Christmas, kid.

That's okay, he said as they descended the stairs and he leant into his father feeling the arm around him, savouring the cigar smoke held in the weave of his clothes. The kitchen was filled with his friends and as they entered the bubble of conversation burst into exaggerated life.

Look who's here, someone said and glasses clinked and chairs were pulled up and he was invited to sit. His mother stood at the window and he smiled at her and waited for her to smile back.

The driver was back behind the wheel of the patrol car, engine idling as he debated staying on the quieter side roads or heading back onto the highway. There was a junction not too far ahead that offered him the option. He lowered his window and listened to the voice on the radio demanding again that he respond with his location. He turned it up, enjoying the dismay and anger as it filled the car and then he pulled out and raced towards the fork in the road up ahead.

The third time his father took him to the strip club, he showed him in to one of the booths at the rear of the building and asked him to wait there.

Your kid? asked the guy who patrolled the back rooms night after night. His father said something that he didn't hear then and they both laughed good-naturedly. He sat there quietly and listened to the music thumping through the walls in insistent bass notes. He had an idea of what was going to happen, but was still startled when the girl appeared through the curtains that sectioned the booth off. She smiled and he noticed the tiny trail of glitter that cascaded down her arms and breasts; as she moved parts of her shimmered.

How are you? she asked and he was suddenly dumb and stupid. Is it your birthday? she asked again, standing very close to him now.

July, he said in a voice that was both reedy and thin and he didn't recognise as his own.

Well, happy birthday for then, she said and started moving over him, her breasts lingering momentarily near his mouth. He felt a lump move in his throat and thought about sitting back, but his head was already pressed up hard against the wall behind him. He could feel the muscles tensing in his skinny legs as his whole body tried to resist the girl's magnetic sway. He was rigid and profoundly scared. The girl seemed oblivious as she grinded herself gently against him. She took his hand and placed it on her breast and he panicked and looked wildly at the No Touching signs pinned up on the walls.

Not for you, silly, she said and sat abruptly on his lap and moved his hand and placed his finger in her mouth and held it there as she looked him straight in the eye. He gasped in spite of himself, all of his energy suddenly stored in his one fingertip as she ran her tongue along its length. She took his other hand and placed that on her other breast and slowed the gyration against his leg. She took her free hand and ran her fingers against his slowly swelling zip.

You like that? she asked conspiratorally, her lips brushing his ear. He felt something come free inside himself as if the contents of his stomach had dropped away and he was suddenly sticky and wet. Before he could even apologise, before he could even speak, the girl was up off his lap and cooing and telling him it was alright. She produced a box of tissues from somewhere and thrust them at him and told him to get himself cleaned up, but not unkindly. Then she kissed him on top of his head like a relative might and left him sitting there feeling *wretched and itchy. His father came in moments later as he sat there mopping at his lap. His father pretended not to notice.*

I'll be done soon, he said. The car's out front, do you want to go and wait for me there?

He nodded that he would and stood up with his hands covering his crotch as if fearing an attack.

Do your coat up, his dad said before disappearing through the curtains.

He sat in the car and watched the pink neon brighten and dim. He was still pressing hopelessly at the hardening patch that was forming on his trousers when something hit the car, setting the alarm off. He looked around startled and saw a man he thought he recognised go bouncing off his door. Embarrassed, he covered his lap, but the man was scrambling away, he was being kicked and pushed along by his father and his friends. They caught up with him at the corner of the club and in the rearview mirror of his father's car he watched as they beat the man to the floor and then kicked at his squirming body. He saw his father stamp his heel down on the man's shin and the man screaming silently, the sound of his agony never making it beyond the sealed windows of his father's car, so instead he convulsed mutely, his reflection rolling from kick to shuddering kick. He looked away and noticed the girl standing in the doorway under the awning watching impassively. He recognised her from the stage, though now she was holding her silver Stetson in front of her and she had what looked like his dad's coat draped over her shoulders. He thought he might go to the man's aid, or call for the ugliness to stop, but she just stood there until his father and his friends had exhausted themselves over the now limp form on the floor. Then when she was completely sure they had finished she turned to go back inside and as she did so she saw him sitting there in the car and smiled at him. It was a smile full of warmth and completely at odds with what they'd both just seen. In spite of himself he waved to her as she disappeared back inside the building.

His father and his men walked past and he could see that they were smiling over a job well done. His father tapped on the window and motioned for him to wind it down.

I won't be a minute, he said and he sounded breathless and excited. Just got a little bit of business to attend to and I'll be right out. You okay? he asked and he nodded that he was. Glad to hear it, champ, said his dad, won't be long and then he was gone through the swinging double doors.

The driver approached the junction and turned on both the siren and lights again and watched the traffic melt away before him as he took the ramp that led on to the highway. He floored the accelerator and felt the car jump around underneath him and then settle into place, hugging the road. Forward, he thought, only forward.

Song 11: Exotic

He couldn't quite remember, but he figured he'd had five or maybe six drinks when she'd come to his table to ask if he wanted a private dance, but he waved her away, he didn't want the company, and flicking through his wallet saw that he couldn't afford it either.

Next time, she called out as she walked away, her brilliant smile glancing back at him over her shoulder. He watched her leave and admired the gleam of her silvery thong, her long, brown ponytail bouncing in a high arch off her shoulders. She was wearing flimsy chaps like none he'd ever seen in a Western and elegant, almost absurdly high heels. Now he thought about it he vaguely remembered her onstage earlier, making her entrance with a glittering Stetson perched on her head. She'd had to throw it on the stage behind her, once the music had picked up and she'd followed along with it, her kicks higher, her hips more pronounced as the beat quickened, her stare dared those in the front to meet her. She was the only source of light moving on the matt black stage. He smiled dreamily and thought about moving seats to be closer. Then he noticed the man standing next to his table. The man's attention was also focused on the stage and he surprised him when he spoke.

You okay, pal? the man asked him. He managed a nod. He suddenly felt sleepy and realised his head was listing a little bit and very close to the table itself.

Long day? the man asked him again. He was looking directly at him now, his hair was brushed back and held in place with some kind of gel, it shone like a puddle of oil shines, his tie was knotted tightly and he looked as though he'd just returned from an important meeting. As he thought all of this, he realised that the man had his hand under his arm and was helping him to his feet and guiding him quite gently to the door. Another man, huge and brooding, with a frame wide enough to cause a brief eclipse came over to help, but the man who was now pretty much holding him up raised a hand to ward him off.

He's no trouble, he said. He just needs to go home. Almost asleep at his table. The huge man lumbered off with a shrug and for a moment he saw the stage again and there was the girl he'd met earlier, she held her Stetson above her head as if she were a cowboy trying to stay atop a bucking steer. Did he imagine that she smiled at him just before he was gently pushed out of the door? He turned to look back, but he was outside and all he saw was the doorman, impassive and unmoving, lounging on a scuffed barstool.

Good night, said the doorman and as he staggered towards the cab rank he knew it was the end of his evening.

She'd left her goodbye note on the fridge. Not even a note really, just a message in coloured plastic letters, some numbers too, like the E with the number 3.

Fuck this and fuck you too Eve it said in a wavering line.

Punctuation, he muttered to himself (it was the kind of mumbled remark that always turned into an argument, usually at the kitchen table for some reason; he blamed his escalating indigestion on Eve's ripe mood swings) then he stared at the 3 at the beginning of Eve for a long time before wiping the message away into a disarrayed rainbow with his hand. An F clattered to the floor making a clicking sound as the magnet bounced out of its plastic holding. He grunted as he kicked it under the cupboard and then he stood on the hollow letter until he heard a crack.

They'd both agreed, no babies, though towards the end (and when was the end, the last screaming match in the bathroom as he stood in the shower, was that the end?) she had decided that she did in fact now want babies. It had become the blunt end of her argument, her one nagging hook in his skin. They rattled cutlery a lot then and she looked at him some mornings as he rose from their bed as if she'd been drugged and he'd done it just to sleep by her side and take something from her.

At night her tight fists would cling to the corners of the bedding as she crunched herself up into a huddle; the edges of the blankets receding like melting snow. He'd come to, his legs bare and a misshapen lump lying next to him. He endured momentarily and then began tugging at her in the half-light, trying to find a vantage point that would free the bedding and upend her on to the floor with a thump. He usually came away with a finger that felt like it would never straighten again. He'd make do by cuddling up close to her prone form, then she'd come to life and wriggle away from his every touch until she reached the end of the mattress and could go no further. There he'd hold on like an infant clenching a balloon, as she sulked her way back to the recesses of sleep.

She left in instalments. The first time she returned she went through the house like a shopper in the sales, fists filled with plastic bags. She thumped around upstairs for a while and then thundered back down so hard that for a moment he thought she'd slipped and fallen. Seeing her again was fraught, naturally, but he had to corral his feelings, he surprised himself not just in the way he had to combat the sadness welling up inside him, but with the dull ache in his dick and the longing that slowly pulsed through his limbs. She slammed the door so hard it sprang back momentarily in a juddering swing and in that moment as she turned they caught each other's eye in the wedge of daylight, the one pulling away from the other and that thing that had connected them both, the inexorable thread, was now stretching, now snapped. Then the click of the door, the simple clunk of the lock and then the silence pooling around his feet as the cat nosed its way past him, head alert, tail twitching a mysterious semaphore.

He'd passed the strip club dozens of times on his commute to and from work. It was out near the airport and on the journey home it glowed dully in the long shadows cast by the highway that ran overhead. It promised dancing girls and liquor in a flashing neon sign that looked underpowered as if the filament was damaged and worn down. He'd first ended out here drinking with some friends after work. He had worn his heartache with a hangdog expression and long, contemplative silences until finally they crowded his cubicle and harangued him out of the door and to a series of bars that ended, with an ever-thinning retinue, at the strip club. He had no idea where everyone was by the time he was gently led out of the door. He wasn't sure how, but he woke the next morning, fully dressed in the chair in his lounge, his shoes neatly placed in the hallway. His answering machine flashed irritably at him with a string of messages. When he sat down to think about it a few hours later he realised that at some point late in the evening he'd moved tables away from his friends on the way back from the bathroom, leaving his case and coat with them. It transpired that he'd come back, forgotten about the people he'd arrived with and found his own table and ordered another drink. They ribbed him about that at work the following week when they'd returned his things.

Man, were you back in the private booths getting lucky? his friends asked. He'd nod silently, forcing a grin and raise a thumb in affirmation, but his eyes never left his computer screen. He remembered he'd called Eve drunk and loathed himself for doing so. He wrote her a letter that he sent to her parents' house, but she'd never replied. A few times he drove slowly past, but had no idea what he might do if she stepped out on the porch and called his name. He briefly imagined the scenario from the Say Anything movie where he stood out on her lawn playing their favourite song from speakers he'd hold aloft above his head. They didn't have a favourite song though and he didn't have speakers big enough. He thought about backing the car up next to the house and opening the doors and playing the stereo loudly, but he knew it wouldn't have the same effect and he worried about her parents' grass. They didn't like him much anyway. Then, much to his own surprise, he found himself down under the highway one night, parking his car near the strip bar. He sat silently and felt the engine cool down. He imagined he saw a shooting star, but realised that it was a domestic flight coming into the airport. He wished on it anyway. If the doorman knew who he was then he didn't show it. He just nodded at him silently as he entered. He didn't recognise the room he was in, though the low stage and some of the haughty-looking waitresses with their giant, circular trays looked familiar. A short brunette girl made a circuit of the stage trying to drum up enthusiasm from the dry-faced men sat in front of her. Her thighs looked taut, the muscles outlined in the spotlight as she made her way slowly to the floor in an exaggerated split and then threw her arms up in the air like a gymnast dismounting. She stood and gave a curt bow and waved. It was a little after six and the stragglers who sat there day after day almost blind and now oblivious to the action were starting to drift away and the evening crowd who replaced them were just coming in.

In transition, he muttered to himself as he found a table near the back and ordered a drink. He tried to pretend that he wasn't waiting for her, but he knew he was. He straightened up almost the instant he spotted her silver cowboy hat circling the stage to disparate whoops and whistles from the thickening crowd at the foot of the stage. That was all he could see though as stragglers filtered in, standing in the space in front of his table peering around in the gloom for a free seat.

Hey, sit down, will ya? he called out to no one in particular, just throwing it off into the throng in front of him, though one man in a black trenchcoat and with a low hairline turned to glare at him. He was worried that the man was about to say something when the guy on the next table called out too; hey, sit down! The man in the trenchcoat turned his attention to him and then the two men were both standing close like they were about to slow dance, bumping their chests and squaring shoulders like prize fighters at a televised weigh-in. The giant of a man he recognised from the other night appeared almost dreamily through the cigarette smoke like a zeppelin that had escaped its mooring and laid a heavy hand on each of the men's shoulders, they both suddenly looked shorter as if gravity had decided to play a cruel trick on them.

Gentlemen, he said, you're spoiling the floorshow for the rest of these people, and they both melted away without a word. The girl in the cowboy hat was miming a lasso and pretending to pull those in the front row towards her. They, in return, were braying lustily and thrusting bills at her. She took off her hat and held it upward and watched it fill with money. She turned, bent seductively over and placed the hat carefully on the floor and pushed it away with the toe of her shoe and then undid the bow at the back of her chaps and snatched them quickly away to more whooping and whistling. She dropped to the floor backwards, he couldn't see how over the heads of those at the front craning their necks for a better view and then he caught sight of her momentarily, she looked like she was humping the floor and then she flipped over and arched her back and thrust her crotch in the air, then bunched her knees up to her breasts and then collapsed back on to the stage like a starfish washed ashore. Then she was back on her feet, legs splayed, leaning towards the audience, then moving sensuously forward in measured steps, just out of reach of the imploring hands before her. He felt a pang of envy and anger that surprised him as someone made a grab for her arm, but she ducked it with a smile and gave the over-eager patron a generous jiggle before she turned and then she too dropped gracefully to the floor to end her set with the splits, one fist held defiantly high.

The next time she asked him if he wanted a private dance he said yes and followed her blindly from his table to a tiny private room in the back. It wasn't much bigger than a toilet stall and had about as much charm. A small lamp cast a dusty umbrella of light and she was suddenly much closer to him than he wanted her to be, he imagined seduction or something like it, but she flicked her head and her hair was in his mouth. Rock music rattled out of a tiny speaker behind him, the bass notes making it vibrate and every so often a face would appear through the curtains that acted as a partition and one of the club's security men would check to see that the no touching rule (written in marker pen on a piece of A4 paper tacked to the wall) was being adhered to. He tried to strike up a conversation, but she just laughed and placed a finger against his lips without missing a single, gyrating beat. As he paid her she placed a lingering hand on his thigh and he felt a stab of delirium rocket through his brain and he found himself sitting back out by the bar finding warmth where his loneliness had been. He'd just stepped out of the club when the large black car pulled up near him and the man with the oil in his hair got out. They nodded at each other.

You good? asked the man.

Thanks for the other night, he replied. Sorry, you know, I was pretty drunk.

I've seen worse, smiled the man as he made for the entrance. He looked back. Looks like we'll make a regular of you yet, he said. The doorman patted him gently on the back as he made his way in.

He was right about that, it went from one night to two to three nights a week. The doormen started to nod hello as he made his way into the club. His friends at work asked where he was running around to at night and soon the rumour spread that he'd found someone new and he let it. He couldn't afford the private dances every time he went there, but he was happy to sit in a space near the back, order drinks from the waitress and wait for her to appear on stage. He found solace and comfort in the routine. She'd stop by and talk to him some nights and try to entice him to come through to the back, but he showed her the open maw of his empty wallet and they'd both laugh and she'd walk away with her glittering chaps riding high on her hips. One night he came in already drunk from another bar that he'd visited after work and when the waitress asked for his drink order he realised that he had no money on him and no money on his card to set up a tab and so he asked if he could just sit quietly for a while and just watch.

You know me, he said to her, feeling dazed and resting his hand on her tray which almost tipped with the weight. She pulled away from him.

I don't know you, pal, she said. You're just another guy.
She must have indicated to someone as there was a man there
quickly helping him to his feet. He tried to resist.

I'm just waiting for someone, he said.

Then wait somewhere else, said the man and gripped his
upper arm. As he was being propelled toward the door he heard
her start up music and tried to wrestle his head around so that
he could at least see her entrance on to the stage. The man
grabbed his jaw and forcibly turned it back so that he was
facing the exit. He saw the man with the oil in the hair regard
him from the end of the bar and offer him just the briefest of
nods. Then he was outside and almost running into a stationary
black car.

He waited until payday until he went back again and loaded
up his wallet with twenties, fives and dollar bills, determined
to enjoy himself. He joined his friends for a drink after work
and when they started asking him about his new girl he fended
them off with jokes and lots of mugging and then he made
his excuses and left. He took his car home, changed his jacket
and ran some wax through his hair and took a bus down to
the end of the freeway and approached the strip club at dusk,
spotting it first between the concrete columns supporting the
rumbling road above. It looked smaller and bleaker than before
and he noticed that half of the sign had finally burnt out and
afforded him only half the welcome.

He patted the doorman cheerily on the arm and the
doorman screwed up his eyes as if deciding if he knew him
or not, before letting him in. He looked around the room, a
beaming smile stuck to his lips. What he came to think of as
his regular table was open and he took it and waited for the

waitress. He didn't recognise her when she did turn up to take his order.

You new? he asked her and she shrugged noncommittally. I come here a lot, I know the guys, you know, he swept an arm towards the open room, but he couldn't be sure who he might be indicating. The waitress looked around and then back at him. Drink? she asked.

At first he didn't recognise her standing there at the end of the bar talking to the man with the oil in his hair. It was like the old joke; he couldn't tell it was her when she had clothes on. She wore her hair down and a short red jacket and black jeans. She said something to the man and went to place her hand on his chest. It looked tender, the sort of touch a lover might give, but the man grabbed her by the wrist and pushed the hand away. She looked down at the floor and then walked through the tables towards him and as she passed him he called out to her. She slowed and looked around; her eyes were glassy and red.

Hey, he said, can't wait to see you dance tonight, and then regretted it almost instantly.

She shot him a fierce look and then softened slightly as she recognised his face through her blur of tears.

Yeah, she said and disappeared into the back room. A thin blonde girl in long PVC boots moved awkwardly around on stage. Someone in the darkness near him began to jeer.

She dropped her Stetson later that night as she leant forward to collect money from those sat at the front. Her features crumpled as it fell from her hand, but someone gathered it up and pushed it back onto the stage with almost all of the money intact. She thanked someone silently and finished her routine with the hat set in front of her. It was unlike her, he thought, and he looked around for someone he could explain the situation to, that she was below par for a reason and, hey, shouldn't they all give her a break? He was pushing down the ice in his drink with a straw when she came over and asked him if he wanted a private dance. She'd been moving from table to table in an almost desultory manner, repeating the question and resigned to the answer whatever it might be, like an unsuccessful salesman moving from door to door. She looked like she wanted to go home.

He snatched at the situation, eager to talk to her and in the back room as she moved slowly and hypnotically before him he whispered urgent questions at her.

You okay? he asked at least half a dozen times, but she remained mute behind her trembling lips.

I saw you with that guy, he said, and then a face appeared in the doorway of the stall.

Hey, said one of the doormen, you're not paying her for the conversation and then he withdrew his head again. He pulled a pen and some paper from his pocket and scribbled his name and number on them and tried to persuade her to take them.

What do you think you're going to do, fucking rescue me from this? she finally said, but she said it quietly. Anyway, it's been twenty minutes, we're done. She was still standing over him and he grabbed at her thighs and tried to pull her down towards him.

I know how you feel, he said, I know how you feel, it happened to me. He was going to tell her how they could both get through it together when she shouted out, her nails digging into his forearms as she tried to free herself.

The face appeared at the curtain again, this time he was angry.

No touching, he shouted, No touching and he rushed in wielding a nightstick and pulling the girl clear he started to strike him around the arms and shoulders and then he was yanked to his feet and dragged through the club to the cheers of a crowd who'd seen this sort of thing before. The two doormen and the man with the oil in his hair got him outside and threw him at the black car; he bounced off its door and onto the floor. They dragged him to the side of the club and he lay there as they rained kicks and punches down on him, while he tried to cover his head. The man with the oil in his hair kept shouting something and trying to pull his arms away so he could smash his boot heel into his chest and face. Eventually they left him lying there, his eye closing in on itself, his nose bleeding and his right hand felt like it had been run over. He stood shakily and started coughing until it bent him double and he was struggling to breathe. There was a bar farther down the street and he made his way there, ducking in the door and into the bathroom. His face looked flatter somehow, his features compressed. He looked at himself in profile and his eye bulged even though it was almost entirely shut. He pulled up a stool at the bar and ordered a beer and a shot. The barman stood back and looked as though he was deciding whether or not to serve him.

Got any money, pal? asked the barman. He reached around with difficulty with his good hand and pulled a crumpled twenty-dollar bill out of his wallet and flattened it very slowly on the bar. He drank quickly and then indicated for two more and tried to resist the impulse to ask the rest of the drinkers

in the bar what they were staring at. He felt like he had a head
the size of a pumpkin; he could barely blame them for looking
over at him. His side felt like it had shattered beneath his skin
and when he slid off his stool to leave all the air went out of
him in one loud gasp. He walked to a store and bought a squat
bottle of whisky and slipped it in his inside pocket. His hand
throbbed as he worked the screw top off and he thought about
tipping the contents on his hand as he'd seen someone do in
a film once. Instead he hid in the shadows of the concrete
columns facing the strip joint and waited for her to appear.
He just wanted her to hear what he had to say and there'd be
no touching, he knew the rules. One more drink and maybe
he'd head back in there, he was sure it must have calmed down
by now, he just needed a moment alone with her and then
he'd make her see.

Chorus

Expect rain, the driver's father would say, and then you'll never be disappointed. If he was going on a date, or watching sports on TV. Rain, his father would say and look up as if he'd just spotted a cloud.

The California sky was dazzling above the stolen patrol car, bleached and cloudless.

And you be careful, his father would caution as he was taking the car out of the garage, you don't know what's around the next corner. His father had been the first to teach him to drive, but his hesitancy on the road, which was at odds with the brutish way his father lived the rest of his life, meant the three times they shared the car it had ended in acrimony and arguments. Once, on what would be their final lesson together, his father left him out by the turnpike, miles from home.

Get out of the fucking car, his father had yelled at him. He'd been maintaining a constant fifty while his father muttered and tutted beside him, his father's hands fists at his side. You think you can slow down for this next corner? his father had asked him. He responded by telling him that he was driving normally and the reason his father didn't think so was because when he was behind the wheel he drove like an old man. Then, quite suddenly, he was standing at the kerb.

I wish it was fucking raining, his father yelled, and then, I'll tell your mother you're going to be late for dinner. It was the last thing he said as he pulled away. His father didn't even like having talk radio on when he was driving. He found the conversation too distracting.

What if you get caught up in what they're saying? he'd ask. Then where are you? He'd picked his father up from the airport once not long after he'd passed his test and on the relatively brief journey from Newark to home, his father had kept slapping his hand down on the dashboard every time he found his son's speed excessive.

Dad, he said, you're going to hurt yourself.

Not as much, replied his father, as if you crash this car, and he readjusted his seat belt for the third time. Oncoming cars would cause his father to tense and whenever he drove him he did so in fear that he would one day grab the wheel and pull it wildly to one side in the face of speeding traffic and they'd end up in a ditch.

I figure you were never the getaway guy, he said to his father once, trying to make a joke. His father only glared at him. Don't talk about that shit, he said gripping the wheel like he might tear it off and hurl it out of the window.

He'd passed his test the first time and his father rewarded him with a vintage Oldsmobile Toronado. It was huge and red and terrifying like only American cars from the 1960s could be and when he sat behind the wheel he instantly worried that he couldn't gauge its width, it seemed to spread out to the horizon and blur against the sky.

Suddenly, he was driving as timidly as his father, terrified that he was going to scrape the wing off and break his dad's heart.

You know, his mother told him once, that's what your father used to drive when he was younger, and he told her he'd guessed as much. His father had seemed happier to have it around than he was. The headlights were hidden away in the hood and his father would sit in the driver's seat and press the button that brought them sedately into life.

Like War of the fucking Worlds, said his dad with a chuckle. You don't get that with Japanese cars.

Dad, he said, you don't even get that with American cars any more. With time, however, his trepidation faded and he began to enjoy the rumble from the engine when he gunned it into life. He'd cruise the rural roads of New Jersey with a back-up can of gas in the boot and scream his way past cars coming the other way. The Toronado drew admiring glances from almost all men his father's age. He'd come out of a gas station, and find men gathered around it murmuring reverentially, or whistling quietly to themselves as if they had just spotted a thousand dollars strewn loosely over the back seat and were trying to figure a way to get in without breaking a window. He didn't keep it long after his father died. Each time he turned the lights on he heard his dad's delighted laughter. When he finally sold it he sat down quickly on the floor and cried.

Dad would have liked this patrol car, he thought, switching lanes and waving genially at the driver who had let him through. The patch of blood on the shirt had congealed and now looked black. He imagined his father hitting the sirens any time he felt as though another driver was too close to his car; using the sound to scare people off. He threw the sirens on for his father and watched as every driver around him instantly seized up in their seats, cars slowed down and heads swivelled nervously around. He nosed his way past them and then flicked the switch to mute his speakers, but the sirens still came. He hit the console with the open palm of his hand, flicked the switch up and down and then realised that the sirens weren't coming from his car, but from the car behind him. Two cars behind him to be precise, the patrol cars weaved in and out of the traffic, their lights glowing red and blue. Suddenly they were the only thing he could see in his mirrors. They were signalling for him to pull over, there were two of them, the one waving frantically at him looked just like the one he'd stabbed and set fire to in his Lexus, he thought, feeling a pang of sadness for the destroyed car. He worked the handgun out from its holster and placed it on the seat next to him, the rifle he pushed onto the floor behind the seat. He'd have to be quick, he thought, pulling off the road onto an off ramp and signalling for the other patrol car to follow him. They sped up and hung close to his car while he scanned the skies and the roads around him for a helicopter or some kind of backup.

Expect rain, his father said.

He spotted a layby where the road was quieter and headed for it as the other patrol car let go its sirens in impatient bursts. In his mirror one of the cops signalled urgently again for him to stop. He pulled in and made to get out of the car to talk like one officer might to another, but through a speaker mounted on the roof they ordered him to stay inside his car. He held up both hands to feign innocence and smiled and then waited for the patrolman to approach. He could see him in the mirror, gun drawn, staring intently at the rear of the car as if looking for signs of damage or for a clue to reveal itself about his identity. Seizing his chance, the driver quickly brought the car into life and reversed into the patrolman, driving him backwards into his own car. He gave out a fractured scream as the car's grille buckled and snapped and then collapsed on to the trunk of the driver's car, his head hitting it with a hollow thud. The driver threw himself from the car, the engine still turning over, and ran towards the second officer who sat dazed. There was blood on his forehead matching the stain on the windshield. The driver drew his gun and started firing as he ran towards him. The first shot broke the glass and missed the patrolman. The second bullet hit him in the chest and he sat back and looked surprised as blood formed in his mouth and coloured his teeth. The driver pulled up level to the car and shot a third and final time through the open window, the patrolman turning to face the bullet as it hit him. The driver went over to the other trapped between the cars. He was moaning quietly with his head to one side and his mouth open. He looked at the driver, but his eyes were opaque like those of an old dog or cat.

Sorry guy, time for you to go, said the driver and shot him in the head. He pulled the gun from the dead man's holster and shoved it in the back of his jeans. He jumped over the fence that bordered the road and started to make his way down a grassy slope that ran to a wall of trees. Behind him he heard a car come screeching to halt, shouting and the sound of radios. He broke through the trees and undergrowth, his head low and his legs churning. He ran hard for almost a mile before he emerged through the treeline, his heart beating loudly in his chest, cobwebs and bugs in his hair. There was a car idling on the quiet road. The car was standing with its door open, its engine making it vibrate. He looked around to see a man standing just in the shadow cast by the bushes. He was taking a piss. He looked down at the wet patch slowly spreading against his leg, his blue jeans turning black against his leg.

Hey, he said. You made me jump.

Sorry, said the driver. He looked around for signs that he was being pursued. Then he stared hungrily at the car. The man was zipping himself up.

They're after me, said the man suddenly and he tapped his temple as he said it. You're not, are you?

They're after me too, said the driver. He paused. Different guys, I guess.

Need a ride? asked the man. You look desperate.

Define desperate, said the driver.

Me, said the man and he was smiling crookedly as he said it.

What's your name? asked the driver.

Jack, said the man, and he tossed him his keys. Do you want to drive?

Song 12: Lucky

He was staring out of the car window, his reflection hanging like a ghost on the landscape as farmland dotted with outbuildings and barns went by. A field opened out before him and cows glanced up slowly, indifferent to the road cutting through. Stupid cows, he mumbled to himself. His father was talking to him again, he was recounting a story about winning, about riding trains and card schools and being richer in the next station than you were in the one before. The miles, as he told it, yielded up dollar after dollar from beneath their clanking wheels as the locomotive pulled and shunted their snaking cars from town to town.

They'd be laughing, his father said, negotiating a busy junction, his head bobbing back and forth with the constant beat of the story, and I was a kid, you know, I was about your age, maybe a little older. His father looked at him as if to gauge the years between them, and those guys, they'd be laughing, he repeated, but you know, soon enough someone would be bitching about something.

A flush, said a voice proudly and he saw his teenage father seated at a table, the youngest face among the four men. The man opposite his father made a fan of his cards like a Geisha girl turned suddenly shy and looking for something to hide behind. The man fanned himself mockingly.

My, he said, I have the vapours. His father pulled the cards from the man's hands and returned them to the pack.

Keep it down, he hissed, but he was smiling as he said it.

Heavens, Lyle, said the man to his father, we're only playing for matches, and then all four men boomed with laughter. The guard entered the carriage and asked for tickets in a voice that sounded like he might be about to break into song. The men quietened down, suddenly they were all business, their heads low as they found fascination with the table top.

What are you now? Seventeen? asked his father. It was nearly midday and the sunshine flooding the car was making him squint. They were headed for the races. Grass and livestock had given way to a small town that had risen up in the shadow of the track. The town was one listless street punctuated by bars and a grocery store. Men looked up at them with as much interest as the cows had. Quiet streets forked off to dead ends and the only movement was the shuffling gait of the men blown gently towards the bell ringing out starts at the edge of town. His father's obligation to his only son was to take him out there twice a week and sit with him in the stands, a paper bowl of nachos on the seat between them as the horses made endless circuits that seemed, to the boy at least, to have neither beginning nor end.

Pick a number, his father would say to him, holding the tip sheet out. He'd stare at the paper as the horses thundered past, their hooves making dust of the dry oval of earth and clay. He heard the thin crowd cheering as they hit the home straight and then he watched as the men around him, their necks still straining to see the result, bunched up the racing slips in their hands and tossed them onto the ground. Then one exhilarated face would come floating through the crowd, smiling stupidly, clutching a stub in their hand and heading to pick up their winnings. It was always a man, though. He never saw women at the track, unless they were behind the barred windows where you placed your bets.

He'll have blown it all by the end of the afternoon, his father said as the man walked dreamily past.

How do you know? he asked his father.

Track always wins, said his father. And he wanted to ask him why they kept coming out here if that was the case, but his father was moving off towards the rail, licking his pencil and making notes in the margins of his newspaper.

Then one day he picked three straight winners from his father's sheet. Strangers were beginning to stare by the third race as his father started punching the air and picking him up to hug him.

Yes, his father said over and over, emphasising the 's' like a cartoon snake. He'd never seen his father so happy and now he too strained to see the horses as their riders pushed them, rounding the final curve of the track and heading towards the main stand. He got the result of the fourth race wrong and his father told him it was just the way it went sometimes and then quickly asked him who he liked in the final meet of the day. When his horse came in first again, his father scooped him up and held him until he struggled self-consciously to break free.

His father dropped him off at home. He'd lived with his mother ever since his father had sold their car to pay off debts.

You're a mess. You're a fucking cliché, Lyle, he had heard his mother shouting at his father through the bedroom floor. The argument moved to the hallway and then his father slammed out of the door as he'd done so many times before, but this time he didn't come back. He stood in the garden briefly and shouted how it was his damn car and his damn house anyway and then he stormed off, he didn't know to where.

How was your father? she asked him now tiredly.

Good, he said. We won. And his mother narrowed her eyes at him.

We won, she said. Did he split the winnings? she asked and then she went into the kitchen where she banged her pots and pans loudly, asking him if he was hungry.

I'm okay, he replied, suddenly wondering why he hadn't seen any of the money.

An old girlfriend who had read up on numerology in one of her magazines told him with some authority that seventeen was the number that represented immortality, and that's just how he felt at seventeen: immortal. He started spending more time with his father, more than he ever had growing up, at the track, sitting in the stands in the blue plastic seats that pinched your sides if you stayed in them too long. He began to study things like form, cross-referencing jockeys and horses and trying to make a science out of luck and chance. His father was impressed. His idea of stacking the odds in their favour was to bring his lucky pencil with him, or if a jockey's silks were his favourite colour: red. Sometimes it was just down to whether he'd remembered to put his left shoe on first in the morning, somehow that was enough to make him feel charmed.

We're beating them at their own game, he'd say, and look around at the other weathered men populating the stands, not like these schmucks. He thought his father might believe it too. Every victory was greeted with a cheer, his father waving his racing programme lustily towards the track, every defeat with a stoic phrase: we'll get them next time, or an excuse: they cut him up at the corner, anyone could see that. Then he'd get exasperated and look wildly around him to see who might agree, but no one met his eyes here, the track was rarely a place where people went to mingle.

His father played at a handful of card schools mainly through necessity. He'd win at one and then return to another to clear his debts there so he could start playing again. They always invited him back. Gamblers always loved someone who lost more than themselves.

I don't welch, he said to his son. His voice chimed with misplaced pride. Remember that.

Even if it means selling your car? he replied, but his father pretended not to hear him. They were on their way to a card game at a friend of his father's garage.

Why the garage? he asked.

His wife doesn't like the smell of the smoke. She doesn't like having the guys in the house, imagine that. He could imagine that, but he kept it to himself. When they got there the first thing he noticed was that all the men sitting around the table looked like his father; worn somehow, past their best.

This is Jack, his dad said, and he waited for one of the men to pull a card from the pack and hold it up and shout, like the card! It didn't take long. Then he watched his father whittle away the small mound of money in front of him as he blundered through one game of poker after another. He had no game face; amazement, happiness and disappointment appeared as clearly as if he were holding up signs declaring his state of mind. The men around him read him as naturally as they did the sports pages and soon they were broke and back in their car, its engine coughing through the back streets of their town.

I didn't play too well back there, said his father as if his son might not have noticed. It comes and goes, you know. He nodded and agreed that it did.

Dad, he said, could you teach me to play, poker, I mean? His dad grinned happily, of course he could, of course he could.

He had learnt to box when he was younger, his father had been home more then and he'd been the one to take him to the gym and introduce him around. He started training three times a week and picked up the rudimentary skills quickly. He knew how to guard against punches, he knew how to build a combination of blows, how to duck and weave, but he never ever got used to being hit. He could draw a diagram in his head (he once made a physical chart on a notepad in his room, creating nonsensical equations; x battled y on the page while he looked for the ultimate solution to solving boxing's mysteries, and dissect where and how the punch had landed, but he couldn't take the hit itself. He'd suddenly be backing off, reeling from the blow, feeling dazed, his mouth full of spit, all his composure lost, his coach shouting at him from ringside. You're running away, he'd spit, running away. He knew he was too. He could talk a good fight, but talk about it was all he could do.

Poker was different. Everyone tried to act remote and cool, but he could see their openings as clearly as he could an uppercut coming. Everyone had a tic, it just depended on how amplified it was, how hard it was to spot. His father's friends were easy, they'd drop their hand down (like some boxers did before they threw a punch, he realised) when they got a card they needed, or blink suddenly, or sit back and try to look assured or nonchalant. He cleaned them out quickly and then had to hear about it from his father when they weren't invited back to the games any more.

Those guys are my friends, his father said.

When they were taking your money, they were, he replied.

Do you know any other games in town? he asked. Ones that you're not attached to?

Maybe, said his father, one or two, but I haven't been back for a while. He sounded sad as he said it.

Card games, he realised, were just like regular sports; you had to work your way up through the leagues, get your name out there, which he started to do as the months passed. He was becoming a name in the Phoenix suburbs and in some of the satellite towns in his State. He thought about playing in sponsored tournaments, maybe travelling to Reno or even up to Vegas, but his father dissuaded him. You'll have to declare your winnings, he said, and the idea of sharing his spoils was too much to bear. His father accompanied him to games, but rarely played any more. He stood off to one side and nursed a beer and watched the game progress as his son's coffers filled up. Some players resented him being there, and accused him of signalling his son or counting the cards. Some would make him leave and go and sit out in his car to wait, but in truth, he would often simply be wondering if he'd given the gambling gene to his son and if so, then how come it had flourished and blossomed in Jack and withered and died within himself?

Someone tried to rob his mother's house one night. He was sleeping deeply as they went through the lounge, grabbing at anything that came to hand. He was dreaming about Billy Joel when it happened. It was Piano Man-era Billy Joel, his hair was high and curly on his head and he wore a blue blazer with the sleeves rolled up and sunglasses that were too big for his face. Joel was showing him how to bluff and when to fold.

I used to play piano in gambling joints. I know, said Joel, shuffling a deck of cards flamboyantly. You've got a good poker face though, he said. Those dead eyes, not like your old man, his face gives everything away.

He was woken by his mother screaming his name and he leapt from his bed and ran to the top of the stairs and when she started shouting about there being a break-in he briefly imagined Billy Joel making off with their TV set. Very little was missing though as his mother, ever the light sleeper, had disturbed them and they'd fled. His father, however, took it as a sign.

It's a warning, he said, paranoia clouding his thoughts. You're winning too much.

How would you know? said his mother. It's not like anyone ever had to warn you off.

He believed in the science of the game and in the body language of the players who played it, not in luck, the elusive, irresistible magic that some people approached it with, seeking out a higher power to help them out. They thought that winning hung above the table like so much cigar smoke. He'd sneer, but even he started looking for talismans once he started losing. He'd lost before, but this streak was as consistent as the winning one had been. One day, like finding the first grey hair, he realised that things had changed; he stopped seeing the inevitable weakness in the way people played. There was no unknowing semaphore being signalled to him and then he was back to feeling like he'd felt years ago when that first punch had landed. He'd suddenly lose his nerve, just looking for a way out. He couldn't bluff any more, and whether it was paranoia or not, he sensed the other players picking up on his fear. He started to make more and more mistakes. He'd fold too early or he'd hold on until it was too late. He found a quarter and it became his lucky quarter; he'd keep it in his front pocket when he played and he'd pat it for assurance when the game was getting away from him. He started his own rituals before he left his mother's house; the lamp in his room was to remain on while he was out playing; if his father was coming to get him, as he inevitably did, then he had to knock three times and three times only and he had to be the one to open the door to him. His mother, who had been exhausted by her husband's slide into ritualistic madness, was happily ignorant of her son's new-found habits so had opened the door to her estranged husband when he'd come to pick Jack up one night. He came running from the bathroom when he realised what had happened and started to scream at her.

You've ruined it, he shouted. I can't win now, and he ran into his room, slamming his door so hard that it shook the frame of their house. She looked at her estranged husband in the cooling silence and recognised what the father had passed down to the son and she quietly closed the door in his face.

The father watched the son from a distance, knowing the terrible feeling of being found out, of sliding ever backwards no matter how hard you dug your fingers in or worked your legs. He tried to talk to his son one night when he was driving him home, but he looked appalled and untrusting; restless in his seat and over two hundred dollars down. Whereas once he'd enter rooms and other players would look unsettled, they now pushed a seat back and made room for him, toasted his arrival. He was slowly becoming the punchline to their jokes.

I'm not like you, he said to his dad, I'm just playing the odds. You can't be a winner every time. His father took his son calling him a loser quietly.

And then one night on the drive back home from another game without resolution or profit he suddenly shouted out and threw a protective arm in front of his father's chest.

Hey, he said, you just ran a stop sign.

The road was quiet. One car came slowly around the corner and drifted past with its window half-open. The car's driver had the radio on.

What are you talking about? asked his father. What stop sign?

The one you just ran, said Jack, exasperated. His father checked behind him and slowly reversed back on the road they'd just driven down. He pulled over and flipped his hazard lights on and looked around.

What stop sign, Jack? he asked. Jack got out of the car and looked around. It was dark now and the car's headlights only emphasised the bewilderment on his face. He walked to the kerb and looked up and down as if angling his head might cause the sign to reveal itself. He walked back to the car avoiding his father's concerned stare.

I'm okay, he said, but he was scared and that night he slept with the bed-clothes pulled up to his chin like he did when he was very young and was afraid of things not seen, but heard, he imagined, somewhere beyond the window.

When he was a young man, before his son had been born and before the fighting and the divorce, Jack's father had lived for a while in a small apartment block in West Hollywood. Chronic gambling losses hadn't yet shaken his self-belief and shown him the fallibility that underpinned his existence. He was still to learn that the infrastructure of his life was rotten, that it was only a matter of time before the beams holding everything in place crumbled to dust. Ashes to ashes, he'd later think as the debts mounted up and the cards stacked themselves against him. That was later though, he was still carefree and drunk and celebrating the turn of those self-same cards when he was pulled over for drunk driving on the Strip.

I'm a winner, he told the policeman as he was ordered out of the car and stood there smiling stupidly. Cars honked their horns at him as they went by, their headlights washing over him, bleaching his features as he swayed delicately. The officer stood in silhouette, taking down his details in a small notepad. He was given a mandatory fine and ordered to attend driving school. The judge didn't even look up as he told him this. Lyle stood there a moment wanting to state his side of things, how he'd only been celebrating his win, when the court clerk took him firmly by the elbow and guided him towards the door. As he turned to go the judge looked up at him. He was hawk-nosed and looked peevish, though his eyes suggested that they might once have looked kindly on things.

The driving school was in a low squat building that acted as a community college in the daytime, and became a warren of night classes and group meetings in the evening. He passed a half dozen open doors with notes taped or pinned to them, offering everything from AA counselling to wine appreciation, which made him smile. He looked at the people inside the rooms and they looked at him, he wondered what purpose or circumstances had drawn or propelled them there. He found his room at the end of the corridor, it was a prefabricated extension tagged on to the original building by the parking lot that was currently covered in regimented rows of red traffic cones. Out there someone was revving their engine furiously before skidding backwards and crushing some cones and scattering others. The cones regained their shape as soon as the wheels had passed over them as if they were designed with accidents in mind, which, he supposed, they must have been. The car idled to a stop and crept forward again and then a man with a clipboard ran forward and hit the car's roof and hood angrily with the board.

Those kids are just learning, they'll get it, said the man who had just walked into the room behind him. He was the only person in the room wearing a tie and a smile so he assumed he must be in charge.

I'm Mr Lee, he said, turning to write the words traffic and school on the board behind him. Someone in the class – they were seated at desks so it really felt like they were freshmen starting a new year – said Hello Mr Lee and everyone turned to look at them.

Now, said Mr Lee, handing out folders, we're all here for a reason, so let's get you all a credit and then back out on the road.

Lyle looked around the room and decided that he didn't want half of these people back on the road. Some of them looked shifty and dangerous, others looked like the only reason they'd want to get their car back was because it was where they lived. Somebody was sleeping at the back of the class, head hanging dangerously back, an arm dangling by their side. Whoever he was he was in a chef's smock that looked oily and damp, his hair hung back in black strands, a hairnet lay on the floor beneath his seat. Lyle decided he'd find out where he worked so he'd never mistakenly go in there to eat.

Must have been a long shift, said Mr Lee, smiling. Could someone wake him, please. The chef was prodded and came to coughing; he looked surprised to see everyone and then made himself busy with the folder in front of him. To avoid getting points on your licence you had to show the State that the rudimentaries of driving weren't lost on you, you knew at what distance to indicate before a junction, not to chug beer at the wheel of your car, how many feet it took to stop if some crazy bastard in front of you suddenly stood on the brakes.

You never know when a child might step out, Mr Lee said on more than one occasion, conjuring up a world where a child waited hidden on every corner for a racing car to crest the hill so that they could throw themselves bodily into the headlights. The State wasn't worried about children in wait though, Lyle thought. It was like the church; all it wanted was an admission of guilt and penance paid. Driving drunk, speeding, letting parking fines pile up, they were all sins to be absolved, come prostrate yourself before the altar of California's traffic laws, Lyle thought. Bow down before Mr Lee because Mr Lee was the conduit and, perhaps most importantly, he truly believed in the message he was sending.

In the break, he went out to the yard among the smokers and took out his pack of cards and practised his finite array of tricks. He shuffled exaggeratedly and dragged the cards out in long curves on the concrete. He drew a small crowd as he always did; it was always good for finding dates, though this time they were mainly a group of people he already knew. They were, for the most part, drunk or dangerous drivers like him who wanted to avoid losing their licence.

Where'd you learn to do that? asked the chef who'd fallen asleep in his hairnet.

Just picked it up, he said casually, checking to see if any of the women standing around him were listening. By the end of the break he had a half dozen of them playing poker for matches.

Poker's fun, one of them said and by the end of the second session of driving school they were playing for dollar bills just to keep things interesting. He was flunking theory, he couldn't believe how much of the highway code he'd forgotten, but was mopping up with each card game. He'd take the bus back home after class and count the wad of bills in his wallet. His fellow drivers provided his pin money and then he'd go out and parlay it into real winnings. At least that was his plan.

It's like you're not trying to pass, Lyle, Mr Lee said to him one day. They were standing in a hallway that smelled and sounded like his old school, every school, he imagined; even the squeak of his sneakers on the vinyl floor could transport him back in time. The daylight coming through the windows was watery and he felt the anticipation of the ringing bell that would fill the corridor and take him to another class. His old friends weren't here though, the only person mooching toward them was someone weighed down with kitchen utensils heading for an advanced cooking class.

Do you need more help? asked Mr Lee. He couldn't help but like Mr Lee. He really seemed to care about his class, he only wanted what was best for him. Mr Lee, he figured, would make a good dad.

Do you have kids? he asked him, but Mr Lee blanched at the question. His brow tightened and he looked indignant and then curious.

Is that meant to be funny? he replied peevishly and that's when Jack's dad realised that Mr Lee was gay.

I didn't mean anything by it, he said. I've got nothing against . . . he let the words go. Mr Lee was a dwindling, squeaking image striding towards the end of the hallway by then. It didn't help matters later when Mr Lee caught their card school playing for money in their break; there was no way he was going to talk his way out of it then.

You failed driving school? asked the judge. Who fails driving school? Lyle leant forward to respond but he was shushed with a raised finger.

I was being rhetorical, he said. I think we all know that I was talking about you. The judge gave a sly smile. Did you win your card game, at least? he asked and then held up his palm. I really don't want you to answer that.

He took the points on his licence and swore to himself that he'd only celebrate victory once he'd got home from here on in. It wasn't a difficult promise to keep. His winning streak began to wane shortly after and he'd often find himself driving home stone sober, his pockets and heart empty, his promising start as a card shark stilled. He didn't know it, but his winning ways were already over. All the sadness and bitterness was ahead of him. He still believed that every next game was the elusive big win. Even at his lowest ebb he would console himself with the thought that he had the redemption of gambling to save him somehow. He didn't realise that gambling had him.

What's wrong with you today? his father asked him as another of his picks lagged behind in the final straight. Once, the track had unified them, brought them together as father and son over a handful of yellow betting slips, but now they bickered and moaned as their stock dwindled and their horses limped home. The card games were no better. They'd argue on the journey home, his father criticising his son's lack of game face.

You're kidding, Jack said, you're an open fucking book when you're at the table. It takes a certain kind of skill to lose that consistently and you've been doing it for years.

Hey, said his father, I taught you how to play this game; you wouldn't even have poker if it wasn't for me. And he knew it was true; that his father had given him the means to fleeting elation, the tools to ruin his life and drive him slowly mad.

Stop, he said, but his father ignored his cries as road signs now seemed to rise out of the street to confound Jack at every turn. At first he thought his son was faking it, using it as an excuse for his losses at the card table, but the obstacles were as real to his son as his failings were to him and they increased with every folded hand and every squandered stake. His highway was littered with signs, the detritus of loss made physical in his mind's eye. The doctor had prescribed anti-depressants, but Jack had flushed them away when they had made him sluggish and dull. Even when he was taking them the figures and signs had still been stood at the roadside when he drove by. Now he'd cross junctions to the blaring of horns and the squealing, hastily turned wheels of other cars as he refused to believe his own eyes. He played his last hand in the smoky garage where he'd started out and when he misjudged what he thought was a bluff and lost the meagre pot in front of him he pushed back from the table and asked his father for the keys to the car, telling him that he needed the last of the money he had in his jacket pocket so that he could play another hand. He let himself out of the side door and watched the smoke follow him out into the night. He started the car and began to drive slowly away. Up ahead he spotted a stop sign and increased his speed and drove straight at it. It wavered, softened and dis-appeared. He passed his mother's house and kept on going in the hope that the distance would stop the pulsing in his head. He clipped another road sign, a real one as it turned out, and laughed as it put a dent in the wing of his father's car. By tomorrow it wouldn't matter, he'd be gone.

Chorus

Why were you running? Jack said to the driver. You terrified me when you came bursting through the trees like that.

Sorry about that, said the driver.

Where you headed? he asked, ignoring the question.

West, I guess, said Jack.

What's there? said the driver.

I don't know, Jack replied and tensed up as he saw a stop sign up ahead. Though he unstiffened when he saw the driver slow down to acknowledge it. The driver let the car idle at the junction and looked both ways down the quiet road. It was getting late in the afternoon and the sky was starting to change colour and the driver suddenly felt tired.

Aren't you curious? he asked Jack.

About what? he said.

The cop's shirt I'm wearing, the stains on my clothes. He looked down at the black smears on his clothes.

I figured you don't want to talk about it, said Jack.

The driver pulled the car out on to the road and pressed down on the accelerator. He opened the window to let the wind play on his face.

Do you know where your journey's going to end? he said to Jack. He shrugged. He didn't know what the driver was talking about.

I'm coming to the end of mine, said the driver.

The two patrolmen were studying the video footage captured from the camera set up on the dashboard of the wrecked patrol car.

The crazy bastard, said one of the cops as he rewound the tape and pressed play. Images of the car backing quickly into the police car flashed up. They saw a figure running towards the car firing his gun and then the slow way he executed the officer trapped between the two cars. The cop's head recoiled with the explosion of smoke from the gun, rising and falling as the bullet entered and exited his skull.

That fucker, said the other cop quietly. We've got him now though, pressing play again, the figure running, screaming towards them firing his gun again and again.

How long did you gamble for? the driver asked Jack. They'd fallen into a stilted kind of conversation as the day wore on, eating up mile after mile of the quiet roads they were travelling on.

Two years maybe? said Jack, it made him uncomfortable to think about it let alone talk about it.

Your dad a gambler too? said the driver. Jack nodded. That's all he was.

Won't he be missing his car? asked the driver. Jack nodded, he guessed so. What did your dad do? he asked.

Spread his pain around, said the driver. He really did, we were all tainted by it.

He looked at the blood. Still am, I guess, he said.

Were you ever a winner? he asked Jack.

Sometimes, at first. I was good at it, I guess. I liked the affirmation, you know, and it came pretty easily to me, and then one day I just stopped winning and that's when I started seeing things, stuff . . . He tailed off, feeling self-conscious and stupid.

What stuff? asked the driver, looking across at him.

Road signs, stop signs, he said, staring down at his hands.

Stop signs, no fucking way, said the driver and let out a low whistle. Is that why you seize up every time we're near a junction? he asked.

I guess, said Jack. They drove in silence for a moment.

I used to keep people in boxes to stop from getting lonely, so I'd always have someone to talk to, said the driver. Kept them down in the basement as if that old fucking house wasn't already filled with enough ghosts.

You're kidding, right? said Jack and he looked at the driver for a change in his expression.

Yeah, said the driver and he laughed. What do you think I am, nuts? And for a moment as he felt the day fading, he missed his friends in the boxes and he wondered what Mona must have thought when she went down into the cellar and let them back into the world. He hoped that they could forgive him.

I'm sorry about the stop signs thing. That's messed up, said the driver.

I ended up going through intersections because I didn't think the stop signs were real, he said. Man, other drivers got really pissed at me. That's why I'm glad you showed up. I don't know how long I could have kept going. I thought it might have stopped when I left home and gave up on the cards, but I still see them, just out of the corner of my eye sometimes, but they're still there, rows and rows of them lining the road, waiting for me.

The driver looked across at him. Are you seeing them now? he asked. Jack nodded and kept his eyes down. The driver patted him on the leg. It was the first time he'd touched another human being in what seemed like an age.

Do you see them on the highway? asked the driver.

Not so much, said Jack. It's like I'm going too fast for them, you know. The driver didn't but he agreed with a nod anyway.

Then let's get on the fucking highway, the driver said. No point putting this off any longer. Let's head home.

The patrol car idled on the highway, the engine's deep thrum the only constant as cars slowed to a halt. He'd spotted it first and then called it in.

We've got a jumper on an overpass on the highway, he'd told dispatch. He looked up at the man clinging to the bridge above him. There was another patrol car on the bridge itself as someone stood close to the edge trying to talk the man down. The traffic had come to a halt, a bottleneck of cars creating a multi-coloured trail along the grey and black of the road. The radio murmured constantly as the patrolman sat there with one door open and his legs stretched out on the road. He wasn't even sure the jump would kill the guy, break his back maybe, but he would have needed speeding cars to get the job done properly. But then imagine the mess they would have to clear up. He'd been working when some lunatic had shot up the highway, but had got there long after he disappeared and the highway had been quiet and empty as the ambulances stood around on the tarmac and *people were cut out of their cars with the jaws of life pulling back the bodywork like someone unwrapping a gift. The machine looked prehistoric and dangerous to him. He imagined it running wild, suddenly throwing cars around the freeway.*

The voice on the radio cautioned him about a possible suspect, provided him with a description and told him to remain alert. He barely took the information in. He couldn't imagine the guy would be stupid enough to be out here on the highway. They didn't even know if he was on foot or in a car any more anyway.

What the fuck, said the driver as the traffic slowed to a standstill in front of him. They'd only been on the highway a matter of minutes before they'd come to a complete stop. He leant on his horn, but stopped when he saw that Jack was staring at him.

Sorry, he said, old habit, it's one of my favourite sounds. He realised how strange that sounded once he'd said it.

And we came on here to avoid the stop signs, said Jack and he smiled.

The driver's shirt was starting to stink and he debated taking it off and tossing it away when he noticed the patrol car behind them and off to one side. He couldn't be sure, but he felt like the cop knew who he was.

Relax, he said, as he looked in the rearview mirror. Jack turned and looked behind him.

Did they make us? asked the driver. He felt sick and the smell of blood was making him nauseous.

I don't think so. The police after you? he asked.

Yep, said the driver. I'd give you the option of getting out, but it's your car and you'd only ended up stranded on the highway. The cars inched forwards and the driver watched the police car moved closer.

The cop kept his sunglasses on and stared across at the car and its passengers.

Think he's clocked the blood? The driver sounded quiet and frantic like a cornered animal. I'm wearing a dead cop's shirt.

Jack looked at him. A dead cop's shirt? he said and the words were thick and repulsive in his mouth.

The driver suddenly pulled up onto the hard shoulder of the road and opened up the engine, cars honking their horns at him as he passed. The police siren started up behind him. For a second he was back in the kidnapper's car, locked away in a box, but then he realised that the cops had never come that day, not when he'd needed them. His father had been his saviour, strong-arming his way to his son's salvation; redemption had come in a bullet and at the end of a blade.

The cop car was coming up behind him and then someone trying to make up time pulled out on to the hard shoulder and followed in the driver's wake. But as he pulled to one side the police went careering into him, causing one of his side windows to explode on impact. It made a booming sound and Jack jumped and turned in his seat to see the patrol car pulling wildly to one side like a steer trying to unseat a rider and scale the banking that bordered the road.

The would-be jumper was slowly being helped back over onto the overpass, someone was holding him and wrapping a blanket around his shoulders.

It's not like it's fucking cold, thought the cop as he waved to the patrol car pulling away above him. He moved onto the highway and had just got the traffic moving again when the voice on his radio told him that the suspect was approaching him at speed. He moved to bring his car across the road and flipped the seal on his holster. He was just about to back up when he saw a car approaching. He jumped behind the open door and steadied his revolver on the roof and took aim. Traffic was moving slowly around him, and drivers and passengers were craning their heads to stare. He did his best to ignore them and drew a bead on the car which suddenly swerved up the grass verge and then back down again, its horn sounding a long note. The sudden noise and movement unnerved him and his gun went off with a sharp snap. He looked at his own hand in shock and then the driver's car collided with the end of his car and caused it to spin violently around, knocking him sideways into the slowly moving traffic.

The driver cheered when the patrol car spun and flipped the cop into the air. He folded awkwardly and then disappeared out of sight.

Ha, you see that? he said to the man. He was exhilarated. I fucking hate cops, he said.

His windshield was cracked and it was then that he realised that Jack was covered in blood. It was only his seat belt that was keeping him upright, the cop's bullet had hit him in the neck. The driver grabbed his shoulder and shook him.

Fuck it, fuck, he said and he pulled the car to an abrupt halt. He got out and ran into the traffic around him and took his gun out. He went over to an SUV just ahead of him that was stuck in the traffic. He waved the gun in the driver's face and pulled him out of his seat and threw him on to the road.

Fucking out! he screamed and he pointed his gun at the cowering man on the ground was almost foetal, his eyes closed and his hands held up to protect his face. It was quiet then as cars came to a halt waiting to see if he'd fire a bullet into the man on the floor. He kicked hard at the man's legs, lashing out at him wildly, throwing his arms out to maintain his balance.

He climbed into the SUV and pulled back onto the hard shoulder, finding a speech radio station, hoping that the words would soothe him. He urged the car forward, the engine straining noisily as he clipped the wings of cars that stood in line bordering the hard shoulder. He felt light-headed and free as he raced towards the first off ramp he saw. On the radio someone was talking about the Pacific tides and he suddenly had the urge to smell the sea and watch the light playing on the water. He used to go to the beach with his family in the summer, his father would wake him early and sometimes he'd be so sleepy that his dad would load him into the car while he was still in his pajamas. He'd wake and the air would have changed. His mouth would taste salty and the car would be filled with the sound of gulls as they rode the currents overhead.

Hey, sleepyhead, his father would say. Let's get you in the water, and they'd walk down to the beach together hand in hand enjoying their shadows stretching out before them.

The driver was on an ocean road, following the contours of the coast. It was quiet out here and he enjoyed the peace. He took a road down towards the beach, descending as the sun began to set. He pulled up on a platform that overlooked the water and sat in the car and looked out at the sea. He was crying as he thought he saw his father's lengthening shadow out there on the shoreline. A man walked up the beach and motioned to him to lower his window.

You can't park here, said the man. His face looked pinched like he was used to delivering bad news. Private beach, he said. You'll have to take the road back out. He indicated the single track he'd just driven down.

The driver leant forward in his seat and pulled the revolver from the back of his jeans. He held it up in profile and showed it to the man.

I have five bullets left, he said. I'd be happy for you to have all of them. Now why don't you take the long walk back up that road *because I'm not going anywhere. The man's features uncoiled and he looked younger suddenly.*

Walk, said the driver and the man did, backwards at first and then he turned and started to run.

Should have shot him, thought the driver, he'll be back and he'll bring people with him, he'll bring the cops. He couldn't stomach killing another man though. He wondered if his father had ever tired of the violence, of the brutality that he'd built his world upon. The times he'd seen him fight or been on the receiving end of one of his enraged attacks he'd been amazed by the buzzing, panting energy he gave off (even through his fingers, even while the air was being kicked out of him), how happily lost he had become in the violence.

His father was out on the water now calling him in. He got out of the car and walked down onto the sand, taking off the bloodstained clothes as he went and dropping them to the sand. He felt the breeze on his skin and shaded his eyes so he could watch the gulls drifting just feet above the incoming waves. His father was up to his waist out there and splashing the surface with his hand. Water was caught in drops in the grey hair of his chest and he was laughing at something.

He felt the water lapping against his calves.

Hey, shouted his dad, where's your Underoos? He indicated his son's naked form standing in the surf. He waded out, then threw himself forward, breaking the surface, the water washing the blood from his limbs, the salt worrying the cuts in his skin. It made him feel cleansed. He stayed submerged and touched the boxes in his basement, heard their voices and felt the life pulsing through them as he reached out to touch them in the darkness. He felt the miles rolling away under his wheels and then he was pushing out further into the Pacific as the sound of police sirens rose from the hill somewhere off towards the shore. His father hugged him. They were in deep now, there was no going back. His father held his face with both hands as someone called to them from up on the hill. It was a warning, he knew.

You're a good kid, said his dad, and he was young again and on the Jersey shore high in the air on his dad's shoulders looking out towards the horizon, squinting in the bright light and wondering what was beyond. There was more shouting from behind him and the quick zing of bullets flying by and he couldn't be sure, but he thought he saw his dad off in the distance, breaking the water with every stroke, his bobbing figure turning and calling him forward with a wave of his glistening arm and he threw himself forward, becoming one with the water as the day darkened and the ocean kept coming.

Endsong

The driver stood in the barely lit office. Above his head bulbs glowed and then burnt out. The sound of typing from the room next door clattered through his head and made his eyes ache. Up ahead, through the maze of boxes and folders he could make out a figure hunched over a giant desk, his features barely lit by a small lamp to his right. He had his sleeves rolled up as if he was really busy, as if there were always things to do. The gloom reminded him of his basement and he took some solace in that. He liked the darkness, he just wished they'd shut up in the next office. It was the kind of high, pealing sound that put his teeth on edge, like biting into the silver paper you used to get with gum.

The man got up from his desk and moved slowly across the room to a tall, wavering column of black and red folders.

As he unfolded himself, the driver could see just how tall he was, he seemed to brush the ceiling and obscure the hundreds of bulbs above him. He pulled down a folder and took out a bundle of neatly tied index cards and then returned the box gently to its place at the top of the pile. He returned to his desk and sat down with a sigh, took a pencil from his pocket and ticked something in the right-hand corner of the card. As he did so another bell rang somewhere, it was clear and warm as it sang and he knew that it was calling for him. And then the giant of a man called him forward as his father once had.

Acknowledgements

These people have helped in one way or another, some still do, so thank you: Mal Peachey, Grant Moon, Sally Haley, Eilidh Duncanson, Willie Dowling, Andy Bass, Dai Edwards, Neil Lach-Szyrma, Dr. Piz, Phill Jupitus (CEO P&P Industries), Lauren Laverne, John Dryland, Lou Pearce, Kory Clarke, Mona Dehghan, Jerry Ewing, Andy Ryan, Dan, Beth and Tom at the office, Mikey Evans, Ma, Dinah and Ron for keeping the home fires burning, Zaki Boulos, Justine Fox, J and Kim, Duncan for the photographs, Michael Forry, Danny Baker, Nicky Wire, Clara Womersley (sorry about all the noise), Richard Thomas, Ralph the Bastard, James Dean Bradfield, Vicki Watson, Adam Channing, Sian Llewellyn, Alexander Milas, Dan Reed, Elizabeth Corlett, Pegi at Rush HQ, Carl Barât and the inestimable Miss Nuala Gallagher. I love Sylvain.

www.vintage-books.co.uk